THE PRODIGAL SISTER

Esther & Jack Enright Mystery
Book Three

David Field

SAPERE
BOOKS

Also in the Esther & Jack Enright Mystery Series
The Gaslight Stalker
The Night Caller
The Slum Reaper
The Posing Playwright
The Mercy Killings
The Jubilee Plot
The Lost Boys

THE PRODIGAL SISTER

Published by Sapere Books.

20 Windermere Drive, Leeds, England, LS17 7UZ,
United Kingdom

saperebooks.com

ISBN: 978-1-912546-57-2

Chapter One

Fred Watkins was part way through a bad shift that was about to get even worse. He and his staff could only conduct the routine inspections of their section of the Great Western Railway track during the hours of darkness, when there were fewer trains thundering between London Paddington and Bristol, and vice-versa. It was difficult enough at the best of times, but tonight it was made even more of a challenge by the aggressive drizzle that soaked his oilskin overcoat, matted his grey hair to his head, and obscured the indifferent light shed by the paraffin lamp he was holding at shoulder height.

It was now shortly after eleven at night, as far as he could deduce from the face of his Albert watch as he held it out close to his fading eyes with slightly shaking hands, so they had at least half an hour before the first of the night mails came hurling along the 'down' line in a cloud of steam. As for the 'up' line along which he was walking, with Bert and Paddy behind him, routinely hitting out sideways with their test hammers, it would see nothing until the milk train from Cheltenham came through at around four am, by which time Fred hoped to be home and dry, tucked up in bed beside Polly with a cup of cocoa to warm his innards.

At least he became free of the incessant drizzle once he stepped gratefully inside the curved brick archway of Kemble Tunnel, a quarter of a mile or so from where they'd begun the inspection under the water tower at the end of the up platform of the local station. Once out of the other end of the four hundred yard brick-sided canyon it would be another half mile in the drenching drizzle until they reached Kemble Wick

Bridge, then they could turn, do the same on the down section during the walk back to Kemble, and call it a night. And *what* a bloody night!

'Good job we bothered,' he yelled back at Paddy Brogan and Bert Cottishall as he caught sight of the bundle in the distance. 'Some bloody fool's dumped some rubbish in here!' It wasn't unusual and sometimes it wasn't just discarded clothing like this looked to be; he'd found farm carts, dead cows and even a bicycle frame on the line from time to time — things that could all derail a train travelling at high speed and cause a major disaster.

As he got closer, there seemed to be more than just a bundle of clothing. He lifted his lantern higher and leaned forward to get a better look, then yelled in horror as he felt his hastily consumed supper rising towards his throat.

It was a woman — or at least, what had once been a woman. Her head looked more like a squashed pumpkin and one of her legs stuck out at an obscene angle where it seemed to have been ripped away from her torso. There was blood all down the front of the light coloured tweed travelling cape that went with the once dressy costume, the long skirt of which was now halfway up her thighs, revealing muddied petticoats and long silken drawers soaked in what was almost certainly more blood.

'Bloody 'Ell,' Bert observed quietly as he drew level with Fred and looked down. It somehow seemed like an understatement.

'Better not touch the lady,' Paddy advised him as he completed the trio.

'Believe me, here's no chance o' me touchin' *that*!' Fred confirmed, 'but since yer so full of advice, run back up the line an' advise the night porter ter telegraph the police sergeant in Kemble.'

Paddy took off, his lantern light lurching and swaying as it got smaller and smaller, disappearing from the tunnel. There was an uneasy silence, until Bert said, 'Shouldn't we move it further away from the line, just in case?'

'No,' Fred insisted. 'The next train's hours away on this side. Yer shouldn't touch things 'til the police arrive, ain't that what we're always bein' told?'

'Right enough,' confirmed Bert, who in truth was no more anxious to touch the blood-sodden bundle than was his superior. The body was fully clear of the line anyway, wedged between it and the tunnel wall, although it was just possible for its clothing to get caught up in the wheels of a passing express as the result of the suction created by a train travelling at high speed.

'She musta bin a jumper,' Bert observed morosely.

'Looks that way,' Fred conceded. Suicides in front of speeding trains, or from bridges over the line, were one of the more common hazards for line inspectors, but they were normally reported direct to the police by their hysterical discoverers, or those who had witnessed the incident, and most of the time railway staff were the last to arrive, after the worst bits had been hastily covered by a police cape. This was a first for Fred, and hopefully his last as well, since retirement was only three years away.

A twitching sound along the rails of the down line alerted them to the approach of the first night mail and they stood well to the far side of the up line as the train clattered and hissed its way through the tunnel in a cloud of sooty hot steam. Since they had nothing better to do after that, Fred sent Bert down to the far end of the tunnel to stand guard, while he awaited the tell-tale sign of lanterns swinging towards him from the end of the station platform a quarter of a mile north of the entrance they had come in through.

It was almost an hour later before Fred saw the dim lights emerging through what had now turned into persistent rain and Paddy returned with the bulky figure of Sergeant Joe Oakley alongside him. Fred was glad that it was Joe and not that young idiot who worked with him in the local police station; not only was Joe more likely to take over responsibility for what lay down the tunnel, but he and Fred were both members of the Kemble Cricket Club, of which Joe was the opening batsman and Fred was now, in his retirement from once having been its wicket keeper, an umpire.

'What yer got fer me?' Joe enquired as he nodded his recognition.

'Down there — a dead woman,' Fred grunted.

'Did yer check that she were dead?' Joe asked routinely.

Fred snorted. 'Take a look fer yerself. Yer won't need no doctor's qualifications ter tell yer she's a goner.'

Fred reluctantly accompanied Joe back inside the tunnel and showed him what he meant. Joe nodded sagely and looked more closely at what was left of the face.

'I figured she were a jumper,' Fred advised him helpfully.

Joe shook his head. 'I 'ope yer examine railway lines more carefully than dead bodies.'

'Funnily enough, I don't get so many o' them in my line o' work as you do,' Fred replied sarcastically, 'but what yer gettin' at?'

Joe stood back up and pointed back down at the pulpy mass above the shoulders. 'She's bin fitted wi' a gag. Take a look in 'er mouth.'

'I'd rather not — but so what?'

'If you was goin' ter jump in front of a train, would yer stuff a gag in yer own mouth?'

'No, likely not. So yer reckon somebody else did that?'

'Seems likely,' Joe confirmed. 'But it don't make sense that someone dragged her down all this way ter shove 'er in front of a train. It'd increase 'er chances o' breakin' free from 'is grasp. Plus, if yer gonna do it in a lonely tunnel, why bother gaggin' 'er in the first place?'

'If yer right, an' she were dragged 'ere from somewhere further up the track, the gag musta bin ter stop 'er screamin' while she were taken 'ere,' Fred suggested.

'Maybe. But my money's on 'er bein' shoved off a movin' train. When were the last express that come through?'

'That'd be the up afternoon "Cornishman" from Penzance. It come through about ten o'clock, when we was just clockin' on fer the night.'

'Nothing since?'

'Only locals, stoppin' at Kemble. The last o' them woulda bin around quarter ter eleven.'

'And where were you then?'

'Just startin' down the track, under the water tower back there.'

'So you weren't in this tunnel at any time before *when*, exactly?'

'When we found the body — musta bin past eleven, why?'

'This unfortunate lady coulda bin pushed from a movin' train and you wouldn't 'ave bin any the wiser, would yer?'

'No, 'course not, but what makes yer think that's what 'appened to 'er?'

'Just a feelin', that's all. We'll maybe know better when the police doctor gets 'ere.'

'An' when's that likely ter be?'

'Not 'til daylight. Looks like yer night shift just became a day shift an' all.'

"Owd'yer mean?'

'Well someone's got ter stay wi' the body 'til they gets 'ere from Swindon. And that won't 'appen 'til I get back ter me office an' telegraph 'em. I can send the boy down ter guard the body itself, but we need folk kept out o' both ends o' the tunnel. That's gonna 'ave ter be you an' a colleague, I'm afraid. It needs a senior man. On me way back, I'll let Polly know what's 'appened, an' that yer'll be late fer yer breakfast.'

It was fully daylight before Fred eased himself up from his haunches, pushed back from the tunnel entrance that he'd been leaning against, half dozing and waved at the small party of men who were approaching from the direction of Kemble Station. The signals were in the horizontal position and there appeared to be a queue of stationary trains waiting on the up line way back beyond Kemble. Meanwhile, the morning traffic was slowly increasing on the down line and those alighting at the very end of the extended platform were almost abreast of Fred and were craning their necks in curiosity.

'I'm Inspector Manly from Swindon,' the tall grey-haired uniformed officer advised Fred as he drew level with him, 'and this is Dr. Bebbington, police surgeon.'

'Has anyone touched the body?' Bebbington enquired.

'You must be jokin',' Fred replied with a surly grimace. 'Just wait 'til yer see it. It's near the far end, down that way.' He indicated with a wave of his hand. The doctor looked anxiously back towards Kemble and Fred knew what he was thinking.

'It's alright,' he assured the doctor. 'They've stopped the trains on this 'alf o' the track, but don't wander over onto the other one, 'cos the down line's still operatin'.'

Back at the body, Dr Bebbington squatted down for a better look, while Fred looked the other way. Meanwhile, Inspector Manly was examining the walls in company with Sergeant Oakley.

'I told yer so,' Oakley yelled back at Fred. 'Take a look at these walls.'

Fred reluctantly walked over to join them and tried to make sense of the scrape marks on the brickwork that Joe was triumphantly pointing at.

'We couldn't see 'em while it were still dark, but yer can see where 'er body caught the sides an' scraped down 'em as she flew outta the carriage. She probably bounced off the wall and under the following carriages, which explains the mess she's in.'

'Yeah, thanks fer that,' Fred muttered. 'I'm not so sure I'll be needin' me breakfast after all.'

The doctor was in the act of closing his medical bag as Fred and Joe walked back towards him and Joe pointed out what he had just discovered.

'Consistent with the visible injuries, anyway,' Dr Bebbington confirmed, 'but I can't tell you anything more until I get her on the table back at the mortuary. Time of death sometime around midnight last night, that's the best I can do at this stage. You can move her now and reopen the line.'

While Constable Jacks went in search of a handcart, Fred hurried back to the station and advised a very relieved stationmaster that the up line could be re-opened to traffic. The small crowd at the ticket window gave a hollow cheer at the news and the stationmaster sent the message to the signalman in the box three hundred yards north of Kemble that he could drop the arm.

Chapter Two

Esther Enright finally felt confident enough to lower baby Lily gently into her cot, then stood back up and held her breath. The child's eyes flickered open for a brief second as she whimpered in feeble protest, then they closed again and Esther sighed with relief. Lily was Esther's first and the new mother was uncertain what one was supposed to do to ease the pain of teething; she knew that some desperate mothers resorted to laudanum, but Alice Bridges, one floor up, had advised her against it. 'Just the warmth an' reassurance of its mother, that's all a bubby needs,' she'd told her, and she'd had two of her own, so perhaps she knew best.

Esther caught her own reflection in the bedside mirror and straightened a few stray wisps of her long black curls. Then she looked down at the unmade bed and Jack's clothes from yesterday that hadn't yet reached the privacy of the laundry basket. As she stripped back the bed sheets and began re-laying them, she reflected on the past two years and the changes that they had brought to her previous humdrum existence running old Isaac Rosen's garment business in Spitalfields, before the man who'd been her unofficial father had died and left the business to her.

Although a skilled seamstress herself, and a recent convert to the book-keeping side of the enterprise, she'd sold the business to a property development company when Jack had proposed marriage and she'd finally given in to the cravings that had been increasingly overtaking her every time she'd been in his company. But before that she'd continued residing in the same building while she assisted the incoming tenant, a union founder who'd finished up being murdered in a vendetta from which Esher herself had barely escaped with her life.

The physical side of marriage proved to be everything Esther had hoped for and more, following their marriage inside the lofty old St Margaret's Church in Jack's boyhood home of Barking. They had a week's blissful honeymoon in a guest house in Southend, before moving officially into their new home to begin their married life together. Although the sale proceeds from the old Rosen building in Lamb Street had been more money than Esther had seen in her entire life, they hadn't seemed so large when compared with the prices of residential accommodation in north London, where Jack needed to live in order to travel daily to and from his detective work in Whitehall's Scotland Yard. Jack was a Detective Constable, working alongside his Detective Sergeant uncle, Percy Enright, who'd coaxed Jack into the police force several years previously, just before the start of the series of prostitute murders in Whitechapel which had first brought Jack and Esther together.

In the end, Jack and Esther had settled for the second floor suite of rooms at 14 Crescent Row, Clerkenwell. Two bedrooms, a living room, a bathroom and a kitchen. A far cry from the rambling four bedroomed house in Barking that Jack had grown up in, but a long way up indeed from the single back room in a Spitalfields lodging house in which Esther had once eked out a modest living as a seamstress. She'd been a single girl in a violent part of London where human life was cheap, and female life even cheaper. Still, at least she'd learned the value of money and was more than able to manage the household on Jack's twenty-four shillings a week, along with the married man's allowance of an additional five shillings, and free coal.

Lillian Rachael Enright had come along just over a year after their marriage, and now, in July 1892, she was cutting her first teeth. Esther had taken to childbirth like a natural and Jack adored little Lily.

With a frisson of alarm, Esther heard their entrance door being opened from the hallway and Jack's cheery shout to announce that he was home. Esther emerged from Lily's bedroom, her fingers on her lips to indicate that she had only just got their daughter to sleep and Jack mouthed an apology as he walked towards her, arms open, and gave her the sort of kiss from which there was usually no return.

'I haven't even given supper a thought,' she confessed in a whisper. 'I've only just got Lily down and it's been one of those days when she bawled every time she wasn't feeding.'

An hour later, as they sat eating up the remains of Sunday's lamb roast and the potatoes that Esther had put on to boil she enquired about Jack's working day.

'Excellent!' he enthused. 'We finally got that brute who's been molesting women on the Embankment.'

'That's good news,' Esther agreed, 'especially for women.'

'Also for Harvey Bennett, who was getting mighty tired of dressing up in women's clothing,' Jack grinned. 'I know some men enjoy it, but not Harvey. Still, that's the price you pay for being the only man in River Division who doesn't have a moustache.'

'So what now?' Esther asked. 'You've been on that Embankment detail for a week or two now, so what does Percy intend to drag you into next? Foiling bank robberies, or hunting down Fenians?'

'No idea,' Jack admitted. 'He was called away to a meeting with Chief Inspector Wallace, who's in charge of country enquiries, so it may be that I have to travel away for a few days.

They've let us work together ever since our success in solving all those union-related burglaries.'

'With my assistance, let me remind you yet again,' Esther added.

'Whoever she turns out to be, she was approximately three months pregnant,' James Bebbington advised the two men from Scotland Yard who'd been called in by the local Swindon force.

'Nothing in her clothing to indicate who she might have been?' Percy Enright asked hopefully.

Bebbington shook his head. 'Only where she'd come from, which deepens the mystery. In her purse was the return half of a rail ticket from London Paddington to Kemble — a small community just north of here, where her body was found in the local railway tunnel. The ticket was dated to the day her body was discovered, which suggests that she may have travelled to Kemble and then for some inexplicable reason taken it into her head to return the same day. There's a laundry mark on one of the undergarments that we believe to be that of a London laundry and the local police have instigated enquiries in that direction, but that's as far as we've got.'

'You believe that the woman may have been in Kemble during the day she died?' Jack asked by way of confirmation. When Bebbington nodded, Jack continued: 'Doesn't that make it much more likely that someone threw her in front of a fast moving train further up the line — perhaps even from the platform itself — and that her body was dragged into the tunnel by the wheels of the locomotive, then became dislodged when it somehow hit the tunnel wall?'

Bebbington looked temporarily bemused and Percy Enright grinned as he enlightened him. 'You must forgive my Detective

Constable, who's also my nephew by the way, but I'm afraid wild speculation runs in the family.'

Bebbington's puzzled expression turned to a smile. 'He may well be right, of course. If the deceased boarded a London-bound train at Kemble, given that the tunnel on the southern side is barely a quarter of a mile from there, the locomotive could barely have got up to any appreciable speed before the woman left the carriage.'

'You're the doctor,' Percy Enright reminded him. 'If the woman was ejected from the carriage at a high velocity, as the result of a massive shove, then bounced off the tunnel brickwork and got dragged under the carriage wheels and thrown back out again, that would explain the mess we're looking down at right now, would it not?'

'More than likely,' the doctor confirmed as he looked back down at the corpse. 'The head took the initial impact, as you can see, to the extent that we can't even determine what she once looked like. That would be more consistent with her hitting the tunnel wall with some force before dropping down onto the track. And the marks on the tunnel sides are consistent with a body having slid down it. Had the initial impact been from train wheels, I'd expect to see far more damage to the torso.'

'It's still pretty horrible.' Jack shuddered as he looked away.

'But still largely intact, except for the almost severed leg,' Dr Bebbington insisted. 'Had the injuries to the lower torso been worse, I'd never have found the foetus in the womb. It's dead now, of course, poor bugger, like it's mother, and before I forget, the rectal temperature confirms my original suspicion that she died at around midnight on the day she was found. Given that she was *found* before midnight, I'd hazard a guess that it had only just happened when the railwaymen found her.'

'We need to speak to them first,' Percy reminded Jack, who nodded. Thanking the doctor for his assistance, Percy and Jack moved outside, where Percy began to load his pipe ahead of lighting it.

'Should we work on your theory that she was thrown from a train?' Jack enquired, 'or my theory that she was shoved in front of one?'

Percy frowned. 'What have I always taught you, young Jack?'

'Never close your eyes to any piece of evidence, just because it doesn't fit your current theory,' Jack repeated.

Percy blew the first smoke from the corner of his mouth in a determined gesture, then smiled. 'And we currently have *two* theories — yours *and* mine. One or other of them will eventually be proved to be correct, but until then we collect all the facts we can, whichever way they point.'

'Starting with the railwaymen?'

'The ones who found the body probably can't give us any more than they gave the local Inspector, and that was two days ago. I think we need to wait until we get something back on that laundry mark — if she was a local woman, then we need to find out what was so urgent as to require her to travel back to London when she'd only just got here. And if she was from out of town — what was she doing travelling here and back in the one day, when the journey takes almost three hours in each direction?'

'Talking of journey times,' Jack reminded him, 'the last train for Paddington that stops here in Swindon leaves in half an hour. Shall we get a cab?'

'You go ahead, Jack,' Percy offered, 'and get back to your beautiful wife and daughter. I'll stay here at the local pub and get away from your Aunt Beattie's stern Temperance lectures on the evils of ale — not to mention her atrocious cooking.

But come back here tomorrow and meet me at the police station where we began today. And you'd better bring some changes of clothing — we may be here for a while.'

Chapter Three

'A little more notice would have been nice,' Esther grumbled as she placed the dish of vegetables on the supper table. 'Most of your shirts are at the laundry and I need to sew up that tear in your grey suit trousers that you assure me you got climbing a fence in Finsbury Park.'

'There's no timetable for violent crime,' Jack told her. 'You should know that from those dreadful Whitechapel murders, and the murder of your former employer not long before we got married.'

'Don't remind me.' Esther shuddered. 'That's twice now.'

'And in both cases, if I'd waited until my shirts were washed and ironed and stopped to check that there were no rips in the seat of my trousers, you wouldn't have lived to become Mrs Enright.' He grinned back in that boyish way of his that always turned her inside out.

'I'll miss you,' she pouted. 'How long will it be for?'

'No idea, at this stage. Probably only a few days, but if I'm not back in a week or so, get the Yard to send their new Dog Squad after me.'

'Don't even joke about it,' Esther complained, then looked up from her supper as there came a heavy knock on the door. 'Alice normally taps politely, so I don't think that's her,' Esther observed absentmindedly.

Jack rose from the table. 'I'll get it.'

He opened the door to a large uniformed constable.

'Constable Jack Enright?'

'That's me.'

'Message from Chief Inspector Wallace at the Yard. Please report to him at eight tomorrow morning, instead of travelling back to Wiltshire.'

'Right, thank you Constable,' Jack replied as he closed the door firmly but politely, then returned to the kitchen, where they'd placed their dining table rather than clutter up the sitting room with it.

'Did I hear correctly?' Esther said hopefully. 'You don't have to join Percy swilling beer tomorrow?'

'We could use you on eavesdropping details,' Jack replied, grinning. 'You have another twenty four hours to repair my grey suit trousers and retrieve my shirts from Mr Fong.'

'Ah yes, come in, Constable,' Chief Inspector Wallace muttered absentmindedly as he looked up from the mountain of paper on his desk. 'Take a seat and tell me how you and Sergeant Enright are progressing down in Swindon.'

'Early days yet, sir,' Jack reminded him. 'We don't know who she is. Or rather, who she *was*.'

'That's probably about to change,' Jack was advised as the Chief Inspector slid a sheet of paper across the desk towards him. 'We got lucky with the laundry company and her name and address are there.'

Jack took the sheet and studied it carefully, then his face broke into a smile.

'Hatton Garden's only a few streets from where I live. Full of diamond merchants.'

'Go to the address and enquire whether or not Mrs — or possibly Miss — Marianne Ormonde is currently missing. Then enquire why she wasn't reported so four days ago.'

'Yes, sir. May I delay travelling back to Swindon for another twenty four hours?'

'Depends how long you need to spend in Hatton Garden, doesn't it? But perhaps best to give your uncle more time to make enquiries at that end in his own individual way. By which I mean sampling every pub in the town.'

'Yes, sir. Anything else?'

'Not really, except don't tread heavily on any toes in Hatton Garden. Those wealthy types are the first to complain about constabulary big boots.'

'Very good, sir. Will I report anything I find directly to you?'

'No, save it for your uncle.'

Less than an hour later, Jack checked the address as he looked up at the expensively painted name board above the window of the art gallery. 'Ormonde's Fine Art' looked imposing and Jack did his best to clean the soles of his boots on the scraper by the front door before ringing the bell that sounded ponderously somewhere behind the double-fronted bay windows displaying portraits and landscapes that would probably each be worth more than a year of Jack's salary.

The door opened and a young woman dressed in a formal black costume with tight ginger curls poking out from under a stylish bonnet looked him up and down uncertainly.

'I'm Detective Constable Enright from Scotland Yard and I'm here about a Marianne Ormonde,' he advised the girl.

'Come in, please,' she invited him with a nervous smile. She showed him to a chair in front of a glass counter, behind which were more paintings on the wall. As he took the proffered seat, she effected the introductions.

'I'm Abigail Prendergast, assistant to Mr Ormonde. Is Marianne in trouble? We haven't seen her since the weekend and Mr Ormonde advises me that she simply disappeared without explanation from their country residence in Wiltshire.'

'Swindon?' Jack enquired.

'Somewhere like that,' Miss Prendergast confirmed. 'I've never been there myself, but Mr Ormonde and his sister spend most weekends there, including last weekend.'

That answered one question, Jack noted mentally. The lady in the tunnel was most likely a *Miss* Ormonde, which meant that he would need to deal tactfully with the matter of her pregnancy. Or perhaps it was best not to mention it at all at this stage. 'Keep your ammunition dry and safely stored away from the enemy', was another of the pieces of advice he'd acquired from Uncle Percy.

'I'll go and get Mr Ormonde,' Miss Prendergast offered, before disappearing through the double doors that presumably led from the front gallery to the office accommodation to the rear. Jack hardly had time to imagine what one of those massive oilscapes of the Scottish Highlands, with hairy cows in the foreground, would look like on his living room wall, when the young woman returned with a tall, aristocratic man in his mid thirties, blue-eyed and ginger moustached, and adjusting a monocle to his right eye.

Jack stood up and was about to introduce himself when the man took the initiative.

'I'm Edgar Ormonde. Have you found my sister?'

'We think we may have done, sir. Could you describe her for me, please?'

'She's dead, isn't she?' Ormonde demanded.

'I'm afraid she may be, sir,' Jack confirmed and Miss Prendergast gave a faint squeak before retreating behind the glass counter, seating herself on a stool and reaching for a handkerchief inside the sleeve of her expensively tailored jacket. 'But what made you think she might be?' Jack enquired, alert to Ormonde's seeming lack of surprise — or, for that matter, concern.

'I'm not stupid, Constable,' Ormonde replied haughtily. 'Your choice of language gave it away. If you'd found her wandering the countryside, or if she was in trouble with the police, you'd know what she looked like and she'd have confirmed her identity to you. You don't, and she didn't, which suggests that she's been found somewhere in circumstances in which polite conversation wasn't possible.'

Jack realised that he was dealing with a very cool, intelligent man. Also a very arrogant one who was used to putting mere tradesmen like Jack in their places. Time to establish his own authority.

'If you could answer my question, please sir, I might be able to confirm the bad news.'

'She was in her late twenties, about five feet two inches in height, with fairish auburn hair and a scar on the outside of her left thigh, some two inches long. She had a minor operation to remove an unsightly mole two or three years ago.'

Jack had no recollection of seeing any operation scar on her thigh, but then he hadn't wanted to look too closely at the bloodied carcass on the dissection table. But he was puzzled that Ormonde was able to identify it so accurately when it was on the left thigh of his adult sister.

'The general description fits, I'm afraid,' Jack confirmed, 'and I gather from Miss Prendergast that she went missing while you were down in Wiltshire for the weekend.'

Ormonde shot Miss Prendergast an angry look, then composed himself as he looked back at Jack and nodded.

'That's correct. She didn't come down to breakfast on Saturday morning. That wasn't particularly unusual for her lately. She seemed to be off her food somewhat and there appeared to be something on her mind for the past few weeks. When she hadn't surfaced by mid-morning, the maid took some coffee up to her room and that's when we discovered that her bed hadn't been slept in.'

'Did you report her absence to the local police, by any chance?'

'Why should we?' Ormonde enquired defensively. 'It wasn't unusual for poor Marianne to go off wandering, usually for a walk around the small lake on our property.'

'The property being where exactly, sir?'

'Sandpool Farm, just outside Tarlton village, in Wiltshire. Not really a farm these days. We bought the property from the estate of the last person to farm it, but the outbuildings were handy for the horses we keep there.'

'And this village you mentioned — "Tarlton", wasn't it? — what's the nearest township to it?'

'That would be Kemble. That's where the railway line runs, anyway.'

'And you would travel to it from Paddington, leaving the train at Kemble?'

'That's correct. If we were in a hurry to get back to London, we'd take our coach to Swindon, where some of the express trains stop. If we wanted to alight at Kemble on our way down, we had to take one of those dreadful "all stations" trains on the Cheltenham service, but that could take hours.'

'So you travelled down there last Friday, as usual?'

'Who told you it was our usual practice?' Ormonde demanded, with another withering glance at the hapless Miss Prendergast.

'Whether it was or not,' Jack insisted, determined not to be overawed by the bullying manner of the man who ought to have been more subdued in the presence of a Scotland Yard detective, 'you travelled to Kemble last Friday?'

'Yes,' Ormonde conceded with bad grace.

'When were you planning to return?'

'Originally on Monday morning, in accordance with our normal practice, why?'

'And did you, despite Miss Ormonde being missing?'

'No, I caught a Sunday train, as it happens — I remembered that I had some business to conduct yesterday. Why do I get the feeling that I'm under suspicion of having murdered my own sister?'

'I don't recall suggesting that she'd been murdered, sir,' Jack replied ominously.

Ormonde shot him a furious look and turned in the direction of the back room, pausing for long enough to bark an instruction to Miss Prendergast. 'Show the constable out, please.'

'I'm afraid he can get a bit heated at times,' Miss Prendergast offered by way of a red-faced apology for her employer's behaviour. 'Probably his artistic temperament.'

'He's an artist?' Jack enquired.

She nodded. 'He was, once. That's one of his portraitures up there,' she added, pointing to a delicate water colour depiction of a young girl who appeared to be lying face-up in a stream of some sort, her head surrounded by flowers that were floating alongside her.

'That's his famous "Ophelia",' she explained. 'She's a character in *Hamlet*. Hamlet's love, and the sister of the fiery Laertes. Shakespeare,' she added, in case the classics were outside the reading range of a police officer.

'She's beautiful,' Jack observed admiringly.

'That's Mr Ormonde's personal favourite and he's very reluctant to sell it, despite offers in the hundreds of pounds. He'll probably be even more reluctant now.'

'Why's that?' Jack asked.

'The model for Ophelia was poor Miss Marianne. I'm surprised he didn't point that out when you were asking for her description.'

Jack looked more carefully at the painting and tried to reconcile the entrancing, slightly misty and wistful, young face in the portrait with the mangled mess he'd been forced to look at in the mortuary.

'Was Miss Ormonde also an artist?' he enquired.

Miss Prendergast shook her head. 'No, she handled the books of account for the business. I do the cataloguing and valuing. I'm a student of art myself — Camberwell.'

'So Miss Marianne's death will create a vacancy for an accounts clerk?' Jack asked, a thought already forming in his mind.

Miss Prendergast winced slightly. 'Nothing so common as an "accounts clerk", I'm afraid. Mr Ormonde was always very particular in describing Miss Marianne's duties as those of a "Financial Controller". You probably gathered already that Mr Ormonde is very particular in *everything*.'

Everything except reporting his missing sister to the local police, Jack reminded himself before moving towards the front door. Then a thought occurred to him; he might get answers from Miss Prendergast that he hadn't wished to put to her employer. 'Do you happen to know if Miss Ormonde had a young man?'

Miss Prendergast blushed slightly at the mere suggestion, then managed a smile. 'If she did, she said nothing to me, but then we didn't exactly exchange confidences. However, I'm sure her brother wouldn't have approved of anything like that — he was very protective where Miss Marianne was concerned.'

'Yes, I can imagine,' Jack replied with faint sarcasm. 'Anyway, thank you for your assistance, Miss Prendergast.'

'Abigail, please,' she replied with a warmer smile and Jack remembered that his boyish charm could sometimes achieve wonders where constabulary sternness failed. A pity he couldn't have charmed Edgar Ormonde into explaining why he seemed to have accepted with such equanimity the death of a dear sister, whose portrait hung in pride of place inside his art emporium. Perhaps the answer lay deep in the Wiltshire countryside.

Chapter Four

'Since you took your time about it, we may as well test the meat pies in here,' Percy advised Jack with a disapproving frown as they sat in the public bar of the 'Artificer', in the centre of Swindon. 'The beer's a bit weak, but drinkable,' he added.

It was the Wednesday following the discovery of Marianne Ormonde's body and Jack was in the process of trying to explain what he'd learned at her brother's art gallery, while Uncle Percy seemed more interested in their accommodation. Jack had left on an early train from Paddington, with a full farewell breakfast cooked by a somewhat tearful Esther, who'd insisted more than once that if his absences were to become a regular feature of their married life, she'd prefer him to earn his living as a coalman. His expertly packed travelling bags — another benefit of life married to Esther — had been unpacked in the only room that the so-called 'hotel' seemed to possess, and the two men were supposed to be exchanging information.

'I have a very strong suspicion that the brother knows more than he's telling us,' Jack told Percy as the pies were delivered by the barmaid, who gave Jack an appraising grin that suggested why the establishment might only have one room available for legitimate travellers.

'So he's an arrogant bugger who doesn't like being questioned by nosy Peelers,' Percy suggested. 'You meet plenty of his type in our job.'

'No, it's more than that,' Jack insisted. 'According to his assistant — a Miss Prendergast — he was very fond and protective of his sister. Yet he showed no emotion when advised that she was dead and he seemed to know that already. Plus he let slip his knowledge that she'd been murdered. And his explanation for leaving Tarlton a day early was unconvincing. His beloved sister had gone missing, he didn't contact the police and he didn't stay on to conduct any extended enquiries into her whereabouts, or what fate may have befallen her.'

'We'll need more than that,' Percy replied as he took another swig of his pint of local bitter, then belched discreetly. 'But no harm in your remaining to suspect him, provided that we continue local enquiries with an open mind.'

'And how are they going?' Jack enquired, to a snort of reply from Percy.

'The blokes who discovered the body haven't been able to add anything, but I haven't yet managed to speak to the night duty porter who should have been issuing and collecting tickets at Kemble Station that evening. It's almost as if he's been avoiding me, and his father was quite rude when I made my third enquiry at the house where he lives with his parents. Name of Parsons — Michael Parsons. Apparently he needs his beauty sleep during the day, or so his father insists.'

'Shall we go back up there around tea time, which is when most night workers are having their breakfast?' Jack asked.

Percy shrugged his shoulders in a non-committal gesture. 'Maybe, but since you're back here and you were the one who interviewed Mr Ormonde, the victim's apparently unconcerned brother, we might get up to that farm of his that you've got the address of. Where is it again?'

'Tarlton, a few miles out of Kemble,' Jack advised him. He consulted his notebook for the precise address. 'Sandpool Farm. We'll need to hire a coach with a local driver.'

'It just so happens that I met one of those yesterday evening, while I was having my supper,' Percy advised him with a smile. 'He apologised profusely for narrowly missing me while he was playing darts over there in a corner and I was weaving my way between the tables on my return from the lavatory out the back. We got talking afterwards and I bought him a drink to confirm that there were no hard feelings. It went on expenses, of course, since it can aid police enquiries no end to have local contacts. If you've finished that pint, that's him over near the door. Shall we?'

'Once I've availed myself of that lavatory you mentioned out the back,' Jack replied, grinning. 'You may consider the local beer to be weak, but you've had more practice than me, and it's only lunchtime.'

By mid-afternoon Percy and Jack were seated alongside each other on a fine brocade settle, while the housekeeper Mrs Bradfield, from the matching armchair, was enjoying the experience of being interviewed by two detectives from the famous Scotland Yard in London.

'There's just me,' she explained, 'and Clarice the maid, what lives in, an' old Bert the gardener, coachman, handyman and owt else what's needed around the place. I does the cookin', but I goes 'ome once the dishes goes on the supper table, an' Clarice does the washin' up.'

'We'll need to speak to both Clarice and Bert in due course,' Jack advised her.

She frowned. 'It's Clarice's afternoon off an' she's no doubt walkin' out with 'er fella. Nice young man, works at the timber mill in town. Swindon that is, not Kemble. As fer Bert, 'e'll likely be in the garden somewhere. D'yer want me to fetch 'im for yers?'

'Not yet,' Percy told her. 'Tell us about last Friday evening.'

'Well, like I said, I went 'ome after the supper were served. Trout, it were,' she added by way of afterthought. 'Trout, followed by apple turnover an' cream. Then I went 'ome, like I said.'

'Did you serve the meal?' Jack enquired.

Mrs Bradfield shook her head. 'No, that were Clarice's job, but there was only one of 'em ate the apple turnover. I remember that, 'cos Clarice come back inter the kitchen an' complained that the master and mistress 'ad some sorta disagreement over the trout — well, not the trout itself, you understand, but while they was eatin' the trout, an' —'

'Any idea what the disagreement was about?' Percy interrupted.

Mrs Bradfield shook her head again. 'No, but maybe Clarice could tell yer. I remember because when the puddin' came back off the table, there were only one portion of it gone, so I took the liberty o' takin' the rest 'ome ter Ted — that's me 'usband.'

'The following morning,' Percy reminded her, before her conversation drifted even further off the point, 'what time did you turn up for duty?'

'Seven o'clock on the dot, as usual,' Mrs Bradfield confirmed. 'I'm cook as well as 'ousekeeper, an' I always cooks the breakfast when the master's 'ome.'

'And when did you become aware that Miss Marianne was missing?' Jack enquired.

She thought for a brief moment, before replying. 'That wouldn'ta bin 'til mid-mornin' sometime. Clarice told me that the mistress 'adn't shown 'er face fer breakfast, an' she an' Bert finished off the kippers an' eggs what I'd cooked, then sometime later Clarice come back downstairs an' told me that 'er bed 'adn't bin slept in. Miss Marianne's, that is. So I went upstairs, an' right enough the bed were untouched.'

'Couldn't she simply have got up before anyone else had stirred, made her bed and then slipped out for a walk or something?' Percy enquired.

Yet again Mrs Bradfield shook her head with certainty. 'No, fer two reasons. The first is that the lazy — well, let's just say that the mistress weren't in the 'abit o' makin' 'er own bed, and what's more, she wears a very distinctive perfume, an' lots of it. "Tuberose" it's called, an' after she's spent the night in 'er room, it fair gasses yer when yer go in there, an' the winders 'as ter be thrown open.'

'When it was realised that she hadn't slept in her room,' Jack persisted, 'what did you all do next?'

'Well, the master went walkin' round the lake, 'cos that's where 'is sister were in the 'abit o' walkin' sometimes, then 'e seemed ter accept that she'd maybe gone further afield an' 'e tried ter assure us that she'd be back in due course.'

'But she wasn't?' Percy prompted her, earning another vigorous shake of the head.

'No, she never come back that day, nor the next.' Her face turned slightly pale, despite her ruddy rural complexion, as she asked, 'Is it true what they're sayin' — that 'er body were found in the railway tunnel at Kemble?'

'I'm afraid so,' Percy confirmed gently and she reached inside the sleeve of her blouse for her handkerchief and blew her nose loudly, adding 'poor lamb', before falling silent.

'Did anyone suggest calling in the local police?' Jack enquired.

'Bert did, but the master said not to create a fuss. Said as 'ow Miss Marianne 'ad a lot o' personal worries an' were gettin' a bit absentminded, like.'

'But surely, you must all have been worried for her safety, wandering the countryside, exposed to the elements and who knows what all else?' Jack insisted.

Mrs Bradfield shrugged in half agreement. 'Like I said, we was — Clarice an' me, anyroad, an' Bert were goin' on about 'ow she coulda met wi' foul play, an' all that, but the master said not ter worry, so we tried not ter.'

'Do you have any idea how she was dressed when she left?' Percy enquired.

Mrs Bradfield nodded for once. 'It just so 'appened that I 'elped 'er unpack 'er things when she first arrived, an' I reckon that she musta put back on the tweed cape she'd bin wearin' when she got 'ere from London, 'cos it's nowhere ter be found now. An' accordin' ter Clarice she 'adn't bothered changin' fer supper, so she'd still 'ave bin wearin' the light brown costume she arrived in. A long gown wi' a matchin' jacket, it were.'

'That suggests that she left here sometime on the Friday evening,' Percy prompted her, 'since it was raining that night, wasn't it?'

'It were just startin' when I left ter go 'ome,' she confirmed. 'More like a drizzle, it were, but I lives a mile down the road, third cottage on the left as yer comin' inter the village, so I was fair soakin' when I finally reached me own back door.'

'You didn't see either her or the master on your journey home?' Percy enquired and it was back to the vigorous head shake.

'Mind you, I 'ad me 'ead down at the time, on account o' the weather, but neither of 'em passed me on the road.'

Percy and Jack exchanged glances and shakes of the head. Jack closed his notebook and stood up, followed by Percy, who stretched out his hand towards the housekeeper, which she gripped with a firmness that suggested years of practice with a rolling pin.

'Thank you for your assistance, Mrs Bradfield,' he cooed in his constabulary manner. 'If there's anything else that occurs to you, please leave a message with Sergeant Oakley at the local station.'

'There's maybe one thing ... no, p'raps I shouldn't mention it.' She hesitated and Percy's look became sterner.

'We're investigating the mysterious death of your former mistress, Mrs Bradfield. If there's anything at all that you think may help us...?'

She stood wringing her hands for a moment, then opened up. 'Well, I'm not one fer talkin' ill o' the dead, yer understand, but it's just...'

'Just what?' Jack prompted her.

'Well, mind when I mentioned Miss Marianne's distinctive perfume and 'ow strong it were?'

'Yes?'

'Well, an' this may mean nothin' yer understand? But it's just that part o' me duties was makin' up the beds in their rooms when they was stayin' over, an' sometimes — not all the time, mind you, but sometimes...'

'Yes?' Percy all but demanded.

'Well, sometimes I could smell it on the pillows in the master's room an' all.'

Chapter Five

'Don't jump to conclusions too early,' Percy warned Jack as they sat in the back of the coach, with the canvas pulled up, on their journey back into Kemble.

'It fits, though,' Jack reminded him. 'The man showed no concern when his sister went missing, he tried to minimise the immediate investigations into her disappearance, he knew she'd been murdered, and now *this* — the fact that he'd been, well...'

'Playing on forbidden turf, you mean?'

'You know what I'm getting at. And she was pregnant,' Jack continued. 'There's our motive.'

'You mean *his* motive,' Percy corrected him. 'The means were presumably conveniently provided by the Great Western Railway, and what we need now is the opportunity. Plus we need a good deal more direct evidence linking him with her death.'

'Do you think he may have been unwise enough to insure her life for a large sum of money?' Jack asked hopefully.

'Why search for another motive, when we've got her pregnancy?'

'But how can we prove that they were ... well, *at it?*' Jack replied.

Percy frowned. 'A very good point. From what you tell me about the man and his manner, he'd hardly be likely to admit it, would he? Apart from the scandal and the social disgrace, it would be pointing the finger at him directly for her death.'

'We need more information about his movements on the Friday evening. Plus hers, of course.'

'What time is it by that splendid gold Hunter that your father bequeathed you? Assuming that it wasn't pawned to pay for your honeymoon, that is.'

Jack took out the fob watch from his waistcoat pocket and studied it carefully. 'A few minutes short of five, why?'

'As you suggested while we were doing battle with those meat pies, Mr Parsons may well be having his breakfast now. What say you that we call in and spoil his appetite?'

'Instead of doing that and being put off our stride by his belligerent father, why not wait until later and catch him at work?'

Percy smiled. 'There are times I'm glad my brother had a son. And we can sink a couple of pints in advance of that, to fortify us against what I fear may be on the supper menu at our hostelry.'

'Yes, sirs, where would you like to go?' the eager-faced young ticket seller asked from behind his glass panel. There was a slot at the foot of it, through which money and tickets could be exchanged and Percy slipped his police badge into it and smiled as the man's face dropped.

'If you're Michael Parsons, we don't need to travel beyond that door there,' Percy advised him with a nod towards the door that led into the office behind the glass. Parsons hastened to unlock the door from the inside and usher them into his official world, then gestured towards a gas stove in the corner.

'I've just put some water on to boil — would you gents like a cuppa?'

'No thank you,' Percy replied sternly. 'Just some information.'

'My father said that the police wanted to speak to me,' Parsons replied with a weak smile. 'I take it that it's about that evening that the woman was found in the tunnel?'

'Unless you've been defrauding the Great Western Railway, then yes, we'll restrict our questions to that. I'm Detective Sergeant Enright and this is my Detective Constable colleague, also called Enright. You may notice the family resemblance, but we're both from Scotland Yard.'

'Delighted, I'm sure,' Parsons replied without releasing the forced smile from his lips. 'So what can I tell you?'

'On the night that the body was found in the tunnel, when did the last train leave Kemble for London Paddington?'

'The last one that stopped here? That would be the ten thirty five — "all stations".'

'And the one before that?' Jack enquired.

'Nine twenty-seven. Same thing, "all stations" from Cheltenham to Paddington.'

'Did either of them have corridors linking the compartments?' Percy enquired.

Parsons shook his head. 'Not the locals — those new-fangled corridor carriages are confined to the express services. The locals are all single compartments.'

'How many of them are First Class?' was Percy's next question.

'Most of them,' Parsons replied. 'A few Third Class, towards the rear, but predominantly First Class.'

'The last train out,' Jack persevered, 'I think you said it was the ten thirty-five. Was it running on time?'

'Yes.'

'Did anyone get on or off at Kemble?' Percy enquired.

'No.'

'And if they had, you'd have noticed?' Percy persisted, noting the rapid movement of the man's throat as he added, 'Because you'd have been on the platform, collecting tickets, wouldn't you?'

'Of course — that's part of my duties.'

'Fine,' Percy concluded as he rose to his feet. 'Thank you — you've been most helpful.'

'Always glad to oblige,' Parsons replied with a relieved expression. 'Are you sure you won't stay for tea?'

'Certain,' Percy confirmed somewhat sternly as he led the way out to the coach that was awaiting them and was on permanent daily commission to Scotland Yard, to the considerable delight of Josh Babbage, proprietor and operator.

'Where next, boss?' he asked.

'The local police station,' Percy announced. 'I need to send a cable to London,' he advised Jack, who was looking a little nonplussed at their hasty departure from Kemble Station.

'I reckon that cove was lying,' Jack observed petulantly.

'I *know* he was,' Percy replied with a smirk. 'But what about? That's the important question.'

'It's important for us to know whether or not Marianne Ormonde got on that train,' Jack reminded him.

Percy allowed himself a knowing smile as he replied, 'Obviously she got on that train. How else could she have finished up in the tunnel?'

'Perhaps her brother dragged her down there — remember the gag in her mouth?'

'I haven't forgotten. But what if the brother got into the same carriage with her, intent on doing her harm, and she began screaming?'

'But Parsons told us that she didn't get on the train and that the carriages had no connecting corridor. No-one could have come to her assistance inside that train, even if she was on it.'

'Inside the train, no. But someone on the platform, perhaps? Someone in a position to instruct the guard to stop the train as the rear carriage went past him?'

'Parsons?'

'Who else?'

'Then why didn't he?'

'We don't know if we're correct in our theory about the gag. But there's another possible explanation.'

'What?'

Percy tapped his nose as the coach stopped outside Kemble Police Station, then smiled his infuriatingly knowing smile.

'Listen and learn, young Jack. Listen and learn.'

Inside the police station, Sergeant Oakley was about to finish for the day, but was more than happy to accommodate his prestigious guests from the Yard in the matter of passing Percy's urgent cable message to Constable Jacks for immediate transmission, along with his second request — this time to Swindon — for all the clothing and possessions of the deceased to be transferred to Kemble.

'I won't keep you from your supper any longer than necessary, Sergeant,' Percy assured him, 'but could you tell me what time you got the urgent message about the body in the tunnel last Friday night?'

Sergeant Oakley consulted his notebook and read from it.

'Constable Jacks hammered on the door of my house at twenty-five minutes after eleven in the evening. It's two doors up from the station and he told me that Patrick Brogan had arrived, all out of breath and wide-eyed, yelling something about a body in the tunnel. I got dressed in a hurry and the two of us — Brogan and me, that is — ran down to the railway.'

Percy shot Jack a triumphant glance before seeking confirmation.

'You're quite sure that you were first alerted by Constable Jacks, who in turn had been alerted by Patrick Brogan running all the way up here?'

'Quite sure, why?'

'Well, Brogan claimed to have called in at the station ticket office and sent you an urgent telegram from there. That's not the way it was, according to you?'

'Of course not — I just told you.'

'Thank you, Sergeant. For the record, there's no criticism of your actions — quite the reverse. We'll be back in the morning, to get any reply from the cable to London, and to examine the deceased's belongings more thoroughly. Until then, where's the best place to eat in Swindon, or maybe here in Kemble?'

'I don't know about Swindon, but there's a place down the road there called "The Coffee Tavern." It's across the road bridge from the station and you've probably seen it in your travels, but if not then your coachman will know it well, since all the coach drivers use it when they're off duty. I'm afraid you'll have to keep quiet about your identities, since it doesn't have a licence, but the proprietor can let you have a pint of the best scrumpy cider you ever tasted and his wife cooks a delicious hotpot until late in the evening. Just tell Ted Bishop — he's the owner — that Joe Oakley sent you and he'll look after you.'

'Excellent,' Percy enthused. 'What time do they close?'

Oakley smirked. 'You're joking, aren't you?'

'Yeah, forget that last question and I'll forget that the local police sergeant's turning a blind eye to an unlicensed establishment serving cider. Depending upon how good the cider is, that is. Come on, Jack, before they run out of hotpot.'

The next morning, looking slightly green around the gills, they were deposited outside Kemble Police Station and were more than ready for the hot sweet tea that Constable Jacks offered to make them while they awaited the arrival of the sergeant and examined the items that had arrived overnight.

'I don't think that poor constable's ever off duty,' Jack croaked as he tested his powers of speech again and vowed to give the local cider a definite miss in future. He was ignored by Percy, who was gloating over the return cable from London and chuckling quietly to himself. Then he tucked it into his waistcoat pocket and took Jack into the back room, where the items found with Marianne Ormonde's body were laid out on a table.

'Very well, young Jack, tell me what you can deduce from all these.'

'Can I leave out the bloodstained clothing?' Jack implored him. 'My stomach's all over the place after that cider you insisted that we try last night.'

'Nothing wrong with the cider,' Percy assured him. 'If your tummy's a bit gippy, blame the hotpot. Now, what can you deduce from the dear departed's belongings?'

Jack tipped the contents of the purse onto the table and sorted through them.

'The return half of the train ticket, plus about five pounds in coins, so robbery was obviously not the motive. The doctor assured us that she hadn't been raped — at least, not recently — and then there's this card from a London clinic.'

'Show me,' Percy requested, then chortled when he read it. 'Devonshire Street, just around the corner from Harley Street, and part of all that medical quackery that Marylebone specialises in. I'd bet half my pension that this Dr. Weinberg does a nice line in abortions, for the right price of course. That's probably not even his real name, and I'd hazard a further guess that any medical diploma displayed on his consulting room wall was purchased by him in Salzburg.'

'The deceased had an appointment with him a few days after she died, according to this card,' Jack observed. 'Perhaps she and her brother argued over her getting an abortion?'

'More than likely,' Percy agreed. 'The important question is whether he was in favour of it, or against it.'

'My money's on the likelihood that he was insisting, and she was resisting,' Jack offered.

'And you may be right. But if you've finished that tea, let's go and get Mr Parsons out of bed, shall we?'

'Why?'

'Read this return cable from London and if you have to ask me a second time I'll recommend your dismissal for incompetence.'

Jack read the cable, whistled softly and hastened outside to join Percy in the cab.

A bleary-eyed Michael Parsons lurched into the open rear doorway of the labourer's cottage that he shared with his parents and looked accusingly at the two police officers. 'I'd only just got to bed,' he complained. 'Can't this wait until later?'

'Perhaps if you step out into the fresh air, it might wake you up, Mr Parsons,' Percy suggested as he gestured towards the centre of the rear yard, where several seats and a matching table sat paying silent testimony to someone's skills with a wood saw and a large tree trunk. They took seats and Percy extracted the cable from his waistcoat pocket.

'Just so that we understand each other, Mr Parsons,' he advised him in a menacing tone, 'I don't take kindly to being lied to, any more than I imagine your employers do. So tell me again, how many people boarded the last train out of Kemble on Friday evening past?'

'None — I told you.'

'And it was running on time?'

'Yes — like I said.'

Percy sighed audibly as his eyes narrowed like a hastily lowered portcullis. 'Funnily enough, the guard on that train — a Mr Herbert Renshaw — advises me that the train was running ten minutes late that evening by the time it reached Kemble.'

Parsons's eyes flickered nervously between Percy and Jack. 'Well, I was speaking in general terms, you understand. Train guards are more particular.'

'Also more observant, it would seem,' Percy added acidly. 'According to Mr Renshaw, a lady in her early to late twenties climbed into a first class carriage towards the rear of the train just before it moved off.'

'I could have missed that, if I was collecting tickets at the time,' Parsons suggested.

Percy sat back slightly and gave Parsons the benefit of a snarling look that Jack hoped never to see aimed at him. 'According to you, nobody got off that particular train,' Percy reminded him. When there was no answer, Percy added quietly, 'You weren't even there, were you?'

'What makes you think that?' was all that Parsons could offer in response, but Percy was all set for the kill.

'Perhaps it's the fact that you missed what happened next, Mr Parsons. While the train was in the process of moving off, a tall man in his mid thirties raced across the platform and dived into a first class carriage. So far as the guard could make out, it was the *same* carriage that the woman had got into seconds earlier. Mr Renshaw remembers the incident particularly, because he was apprehensive that the man might fall between the carriage and the edge of the platform, and was all set to stop the train with his brake. If he had done so, we believe that Miss Ormonde would still be alive today.'

It fell deathly quiet and Jack was beginning to feel sorry for the young man when his response caused him to take out his notebook in sheer amazement. 'Alright, you've got me. I wasn't there that night. At least, not the whole shift.'

'And where were you?'

'Down at a place called "The Coffee Tavern". It's the other side of the bridge from the station.'

'Yes, we know where you mean,' Percy assured him. 'Enjoying a mug of the local cider, were we?'

'No, a card game. A few of us meet up there regularly and I've had a run of bad luck recently, so I owed a fair bit to several of the men who I play with. They insisted on me attending the game, else they'd tell my father about my debts, and well, to be honest with you, nobody's really to know whether you're on night duty or not. You're supposed to check the tickets when they get off at Kemble, but nobody's likely to complain if you don't, and once you're pretty certain that no-one needs to buy a ticket to board the last train, you can simply slip away, like I did that night. But I was back by one-thirty, honestly.'

'That explains why Mr Brogan had to run all the way to the police station in order to report the finding of the body, because you weren't at your post to telegraph it, doesn't it?'

'Yes,' Parsons agreed with a shamefaced look. 'But if she was already dead, what harm did it do?'

'Irreparable harm to your career with the Great Western Railway, anyway,' Percy sneered back as he began to rise to his feet.

'Please!' Parsons begged him. 'I really need that job and Father will throw me out on my ear if I'm dismissed for dishonesty.'

'You wouldn't believe how many times I hear that from people I've run in for fraud,' Percy advised him with a cold smile as he looked down at him. 'And my answer's always the same — you should have thought about that before crossing the line. Quite literally, in your case, of course.'

'I *did* see the woman, if that helps!' Parsons all but yelled in desperation and Percy resumed his seat.

'You saw her on the platform, getting on board the train, you mean?' he enquired.

Parsons shook his head. 'Not then — just before the last train arrived. I'd closed the booking office and was walking through the forecourt when I saw this young woman come walking quickly down the road from Kemble. She called out to me, asking if the last train had gone, and I told her no and asked if she needed a ticket. She told me that she had a return to London and so I bid her good evening and went on across the bridge to the Tavern.'

'What did she look like?' Jack enquired, pencil poised over his notebook.

'Like your colleague just said — twentyish, wearing a light coloured cloak of some sort and a long skirted light coloured costume. I knew her by sight anyway, since she comes through Kemble most weekends with a man, presumably her husband. They always come and go in the coach that old Bert Gregson drives, so I reckon she must be one of those who bought the old farm the other side of Tarlton, where Bert works.'

'But you didn't see any man with her this time?' Percy pressed him.

'Not then, no. There *was* a man — or at least, I think it must have been a man, to judge by the weight of his footsteps. I heard him running in the same direction from which the girl had come, but I couldn't see anyone because of the dark and the rain. Anyway, since he'd have been too late to buy a ticket and I could hear the up train approaching from down near the signal box, I just kept walking.'

Jack had been listening intently and in the hope that he hadn't misheard he kept probing. 'The man who normally travels to Tarlton with the girl — you said that you didn't see him "then". Do I take it from what you said that you saw him sometime later?'

Percy shot Jack an appreciative smile and looked invitingly back at Parsons, who nodded.

'Yes, but it was much later that same night. We'd finished our card game when he came into The Tavern looking for Tom Bedder. He's a carrier who runs a local business and he'd been one of those playing cards with us. He normally gives us a lift back into Kemble from The Tavern but the man we're talking about offered Tom three quid to take him to Tarlton.'

'What time was this?' Percy enquired eagerly and Parsons screwed up his face in concentration.

'It must have been after one in the morning. I was dropped off back at the station and I remember that it was one-thirty, or near enough, when I got back into my office.'

'Just a bit more information and then we might consider not telling your employers what you were up to that night,' Percy offered. 'The next station north of here where you can alight from a London-bound train is Swindon, yes?'

'Yes, that's right.'

'And are there any trains that stop at Swindon coming back south — that is, away from London — that stop in Kemble after midnight?'

'No — why?'

'Follow me through this,' Percy urged him. 'If I caught the last train from Kemble to London, then for some reason decided to get off at Swindon and come back, is there a train I could get on?'

'Not at that time of night, no. The first train south from Swindon would depart Swindon at around five am, so far as I can recall — certainly not midnight, or even one am.'

'So, if it were you, stuck in Swindon at midnight, how would you get back to Kemble?'

'I'd hire a cab. There's an all-night cab rank in the station forecourt at Swindon. It wouldn't be cheap, mind you.'

'Thank you, Mr Parsons.' Percy smiled for the first time. 'You've been most helpful — eventually. So helpful, in fact, that you may rest secure in your duties at Kemble Station unless you're foolish enough to be absent from duty on a future occasion.'

Parsons was almost shedding tears of gratitude as Percy and Jack climbed back into their hired cab and Percy ordered Josh Babbage to drive them to Sandpool Farm.

'We've got him!' Jack muttered excitedly, then looked at the quizzical expression on Percy's face, before he added, 'Haven't we?'

Percy shook his head as firmly as his persistent hangover permitted. 'We can't expect the guard on the train to be able to identify Ormonde,' he cautioned. 'It was night-time, it was raining, he saw the man side-on for a few brief seconds and he was more concerned about where his legs were going. He could give us the general "type" and that would fit Ormonde, but that's about all.'

'But we've got him travelling back from Swindon, surely?'

'We'll know that when we speak to the cab driver from Swindon, always supposing that we can find him. And in the hope that he can identify him. We'll need Ormonde's photograph for that, I imagine.'

'But we've got him being taken back to the farm from Kemble,' Jack insisted.

Percy inclined his head sideways. 'If you'd been out visiting a lady friend late at night and Esther was waiting up for you, demanding to know why you were so late, you'd have an excuse ready, wouldn't you?'

'Of course, not that that would ever happen.'

'Well, don't think that Ormonde won't have thought up some valid reason for being out late at night in Kemble. He'll know that he can be identified as the man getting a lift from the local carrier, remember.'

Jack fell silent for a moment and was obviously thinking deeply.

'Go on, then — ask me,' Percy invited him with a grin.

'Ask you what?'

'Ask me if I've ever had to invent an excuse to satisfy your Aunt Beattie. The answer's yes, but not for the reason you're imagining.'

Jack chuckled, then he frowned. 'I was actually wondering why, if he already had a cab from Swindon, Ormonde needed another one from Kemble.'

'That was bothering me, as well. But right now, let's see if the remaining servants at the farm can shed further light on Ormonde's movements on the night in question.'

An hour later they were seated in the summer house on the back lawn of Sandpool Farm, talking to Bert Gregson and Clarice Battersby. Clarice, a ruddy cheeked girl in her late teens who looked like a farmer's daughter and would shortly become a millworker's wife, had served them all home-made lemonade from a tall glass jug and Jack and Percy were each on their second glass, chasing the dehydration from the previous night, as she explained the household routine as it had been on the night that 'Miss Marianne' disappeared.

'I remember the barny they 'ad while they was eatin' the salmon,' she recalled as her big brown eyes surveyed the middle distance. 'The master were on about 'ow it were bad manners ter break an appointment an' she replied that she'd done it anyway, an' what business were it of 'is. Then 'e replied an' said she'd 'ad no business ter do it wi'out consultin' 'im first, an' she fair lost the rag wi' 'im, told 'im that she'd 'ad enough of 'im rulin' 'er life, then got up from the table, threw 'er napkin on the floor an' stormed off ter 'er room.'

'What was his reaction to that?' Jack enquired, having correctly sensed that his boyish charm would achieve more than Percy's more formal manner, which was best reserved for Bert Gregson.

Clarice giggled and resumed her account of events. 'He yelled after 'er that she'd regret it an' ter think o' the scandal, an' she yelled back from the staircase that she'd make sure that most o' the scandal would land in 'is lap, since it were 'is fault fer bein' so careless, an' then she were gone inter 'er room an' I never saw 'er no more.'

'Your room's on the top floor?' Jack asked.

She nodded. 'The attic, more like, an' a real cold 'ole in the winter.'

'Do you get to hear much from up there?' he persisted.

She blushed. 'I'd 'ear bedroom doors goin' open an' shut durin' the night, but I always assumed they was goin' down ter the outside lavvie. 'As Mrs Bradfield mentioned 'er suspicions on that score?'

'Yes, she has,' Jack said reassuringly, 'but we're only interested in what you may have heard on the night that Miss Marianne went missing.'

'I never 'eard nothin' once I got ter bed,' Clarice assured him and Jack let it drop.

It was Percy who picked up the thread. 'You mentioned the outside lavatory, Clarice. If someone needed to leave the house during the night, what arrangement was there regarding the key to the back door?'

'There was a spare 'angin' on a 'ook near the door,' she advised him, 'an' anyone goin' out was supposed ter take it wi' 'em, so as not ter lock 'emselves out. The lock clicks to once the back door's shut, yer see, an' there's always the risk o' the wind blowin' it shut.'

'So anyone wanting to leave the house during the night could simply slip out through the back door and pull it lockfast behind them?' Percy asked and Clarice nodded.

'But you heard nothing that night?' Jack confirmed and she shook her head again.

'But it wouldn't 'ave seemed unusual if I 'ad,' she reminded them.

Percy turned his gaze towards Bert. 'You sleep above the coach house and stable block, that right?'

'Aye, that's right,' Bert confirmed.

'And you heard nothing that night?'

''Fraid not, but I'm an 'eavy sleeper, me. Once me 'ead goes down, that's it 'til next mornin', when the birds wake me wi' their chatter. But the next mornin' were a bit odd, come ter think of it.'

'In what way?' Percy enquired.

'Well,' Bert continued, 'I were lyin' in me bed, about one in the mornin' it woulda bin, which were a bit unusual for me. I 'eard someone rattlin' the back door ter the 'ouse. I looked out an' it were the master. Claimed 'e'd forgotten ter take the back door key when he went out ter use the lavvie, so I let 'im in wi' me own key. I've always 'ad a spare o' me own, so's I can get at the gardenin' tools what we keep in the back scullery. The funny thing were that the other spare key weren't there, be'ind the door, like Clarice explained. An' if the master'd only gone out ter use the lavvie, why were 'e wearin' 'is walkin' out coat, an' why were 'is coat all damp when I took it off 'im?'

'The coat he'd normally wear for travelling?' Percy prompted him.

Bert nodded before adding to his account of events. 'But 'e weren't wearin' 'is normal 'at — one o' them "deerstalker" things. 'E always wore it while 'e were down 'ere, if 'e went out anywhere.'

'I gather that you would take the master and mistress to and from the station in the coach?' Jack suggested.

Bert nodded. 'Every Friday evenin', the five thirteen from London, an' then back on either the Sunday or the Monday. Sometimes they went all the way ter Swindon, ter catch a faster train, but most times it were Kemble.'

'Thank you, both of you,' Percy said, by way of concluding the conversation. 'I don't think we need keep you from your duties any longer — and thank you again for the lemonade, Miss Battersby.'

'What next?' Jack asked as they took the coach back to Swindon.

Percy frowned. 'I don't know about you, but after that heavy night on the cider, I'm more than happy to settle for an early night at our hostelry and hopefully something edible to soak up the local beer.'

'I think I'll give the beer a miss,' Jack grimaced, 'but what do you have in mind for tomorrow?'

'I think we'll try and find that coach driver who brought Ormonde back to Kemble,' Percy suggested.

Jack nodded his agreement. Then, after a few moments deep in thought, he said, 'Then can we go back to London?'

Percy smiled. 'I remember my young married days, so maybe you can go, and I'll keep going here.'

'We've no one left to interview, have we?'

Percy looked thoughtfully out of the side of the coach as it took the main road out of Kemble towards Swindon. 'That'll depend on what the coachman in Swindon has to tell us, won't it?'

Chapter Six

Just before noon the following day, by dint of some constabulary weight-throwing and some 'inside' assistance from Josh Babbage, Jack and Percy had identified the coach driver who took Edgar Ormond from Swindon back to Kemble on the night of the murder. His name was John Savage and he was happy to be fed pints of local beer and the occasional crisp new banknote while he recalled the unusual fare he'd picked up that night.

'A regular city gent, 'e were, all monocle an' hoighty toighty talk. I were just about ready ter call it a night, since the last express 'ad gone through some time since, an' then out 'e steps from the station, no luggage, nor nothin'. 'E weren't even wearin' no 'at, so I figured 'e probably 'adn't come from London or anywhere posh.'

'If I might stop you there for a moment, Mr Savage,' Percy said as he slid another pound note across the table, 'do you recall if there were any train arrivals just before this man hired your cab?'

'Yeah, the last one fer London. The Cheltenham local that departs around eleven thirty. It 'ad just pulled inter the platform when this gent come runnin' out, like he were chasin' someone, only 'e weren't, obviously. Then 'e sees me sittin' up be'ind the 'oss an' 'e offers me a tenner ter take 'im ter Kemble.'

'Only to Kemble?' Percy asked.

Savage nodded.

'And you say he was not wearing any hat?' Jack enquired.

Savage nodded again. 'I though it were a bit peculiar, like, since it'd bin rainin' earlier an' since 'e didn't 'ave no luggage I figured ' couldn't 'ave come far. Well, I takes 'im ter Kemble — an' here's the funny bit — when we gets there, 'e asks me ter drop 'im off at the station. I thought it were odd, since there's no more trains at that time o' night, but a tenner's a tenner, so I kept me mouth shut an' just bid 'im a good night.'

'As you drove away, where was he?' Percy asked eagerly.

Savage shrugged his shoulders. 'Just where I'd left 'im, 'cept 'e were lookin' down at the ground, like 'e'd dropped somethin'. That were in the forecourt, where the coaches drop an' pick up passengers.'

'Did you see him pick anything up?' Jack asked.

Savage shook his head.

'Finally,' Percy enquired as he pushed another pound note across the table, 'do you think you'd know this man if you saw him again?'

'Definitely, since 'e were very distinctive. A tall bloke — in his late thirties, I'd reckon. Fairish 'air an' one o' they posh moustaches like yer see on royalty. An' 'e were playin' wi' one o' they monocle thingies, on the end've a string. Yer know — what posh folks puts over their eye, instead o' proper glasses like poor folk 'as ter use.'

'Ormonde was wearing a monocle when I spoke to him,' Jack advised Percy excitedly as Savage took his departure and they got up to leave.

'Sounds like he left something behind at Kemble Station when he was chasing his sister to the train,' Percy mused out loud. 'I wonder if it finished up in the Left Luggage Office.'

'Back to Mr Parsons?' Jack asked.

'Later, maybe. Right now we need to think of some way of getting a photograph of our Mr Ormonde that we can show to Savage, before we go assuming too much.'

'Can't we get someone to wait outside his business premises and catch him unawares?'

Percy smiled. 'You've obviously had little to do with the business of photography. You need to set up a tripod with a black cloth over it, then set what they call the "focus". And the so-called "subject" has to remain still for at least thirty seconds. Then it all depends on the light, and other things as well.'

'How do you know so much about it?'

'Every few years we have a Divisional photograph taken inside the main canteen at the Yard. Which reminds me, we must be due our next one soon, and then you'll see what I mean. The sort of photograph I'm talking about will need to be one of those fancy ones taken in a proper photographic studio. Any ideas?'

'Uncle Percy, let me put this idea to you. It first began to form when I learned that Marianne Ormonde used to do the accounts for her brother's business. He must be needing a replacement and it just so happens that I know someone with experience in book-keeping.'

'I wonder who that might be?' Percy said sarcastically.

'Someone we've worked with before, who's not afraid of getting involved in undercover work and who's bored sitting at home nursing a young child.'

Percy thought for a brief moment, then shook his head. 'You obviously have in mind that lovely wife of yours, but forget it. We're dealing with a very resourceful and very evil man who thought nothing of pushing his sister off a moving train. You wouldn't seriously want to expose your lovely Esther to a brute like that, would you? Remember that she's twice before narrowly escaped death while working for us.'

'She'd be safe enough, just doing his books. But she'd be in a position to get further information about him that could fill out our case. You said yourself that we need more to link him directly with the murder. Her first job can be to get hold of a photograph of him.'

'Do you think she'd even agree?' Percy enquired doubtfully.

'Let me go home this afternoon, then come over to our place for supper tomorrow,' Jack returned, confidently.

Chapter Seven

Esther's heart leapt as she heard the key turning in the outside lock and she rushed down the hallway into Jack's arms, almost knocking him back through the open doorway as she pressed herself up to him.

'There's nothing in the pantry, so go and sit in the living room while I go around to the shops and see what's left.'

'Please avoid meat pies at all costs,' Jack begged her, 'since I just spent three days living on them. Poor Uncle Percy's still there, I'm afraid, but he hopes to be back tomorrow.'

'What about you? Are you home for good?'

'For the next few days at least. I have a short job to do around the middle of the day, but otherwise I've got the whole of tomorrow free.'

'We could take Lily in her pram down to the park, or even further afield — maybe to visit your mother,' Esther suggested.

Jack shook his head. 'I value my time at home with you too much. A long lie-in, then I'll bring you tea and toast in bed, then we can — well, we'll see what comes up, shall we?'

'You know as well as I do what'll come up, Jack Enright,' Esther teased him.

'You're getting worse than me, you shameless married woman, you.'

'That must be the result of being pregnant again,' she whispered hoarsely.

Jack turned round quickly, his eyes wide open and a massive grin from ear to ear. 'Really?'

'Really, according to Dr. Penfold, who we owe six shillings to, by the way. I didn't have any change in my purse and his girl refused to break my only remaining five pound note.'

'Give it to me and I'll go and get some cockles from the stall on the corner. Then tomorrow evening, I'll cook supper while you sit with your feet up.'

'Feet up where?' she joked.

He chuckled with sheer excitement and pleasure as he hugged her to him. 'Dearest, darling Esther, I'm *so* excited by your news! I love you *so* much — you make me so happy!'

Lily began protesting from the next room and Esther pushed Jack away with a smile.

'So demonstrate your happiness by going and collecting your daughter and bringing her in here. Tell her that the milk counter's open for business. And before the next one's born, learn how to breast feed.'

Jack's apprehension that he might have to spend the entire day walking up and down Hatton Garden was dispelled when after only half an hour the front door opened and out walked Miss Prendergast, carrying a wicker shopping basket and heading in the direction of Charterhouse Street.

Jack crossed the road and walked along behind her, slowly quickening his pace until he could pretend that their encounter was entirely fortuitous as he called out, 'It's Abigail, isn't it?'

She stopped, turned and smiled back at the boyish grin that never failed.

'Aren't you the ... the...?'

'That's me — Constable Enright. But call me Jack. I called in to speak to your employer on Tuesday.'

'Are you back to see him again?'

'If I were, I wouldn't be walking past his premises, would I? It happens to be my day off and I was taking the air. I live only a few streets away, in Clerkenwell. May I walk with you?'

'Of course. I'm on my way down to the omnibus stop, then into Holborn for some stationery supplies. And perhaps some more art paper while I'm at it, although I hardly have time these days.'

'Is Mr Ormonde keeping you busy?'

'He most certainly is, although the pittance he pays me he's got a cheek. Now that Miss Marianne's gone he seems to think that I can manage the accounts as well as the catalogues. I keep telling him, I'm an artist, not a bookkeeper, and just between ourselves I think he's beginning to lose patience with me.'

'So is he advertising for a replacement for Miss Marianne?'

Abigail snorted daintily. 'Mr Ormonde do something as vulgar as advertise for servants? My goodness me, what would the world be coming to if he lowered himself to do that?'

'May I carry your basket?' Jack asked, doing his best impersonation of a love-struck young man seeking to curry favour with a lady who had attracted his affections.

'It's alright, my bus stop's just up ahead, but you can stay and talk with me until the bus arrives, if you wish.'

'Thank you,' Jack responded with what he hoped was a grateful smile. 'So how has Mr Ormonde taken to the news that his sister died tragically?'

Another dainty snort. 'I think he'd be more emotional if he lost out on an auction bid for a minor Impressionist work. It's as if she never existed. If I were him, I couldn't bear to look at the "Ophelia" on the wall, since it's such a reminder of poor Marianne, but it's still in pride of place behind the counter. Perhaps now he'll sell it — who knows? Anyway, I think that's my bus, so thank you for your company and any day that you feel like taking the air again, I normally take an hour off at around one o'clock and go for a walk around the block.'

'I'll be sure to do that,' Jack replied with another practised grin, then smiled more meaningfully as he turned back towards home, muttering, 'Candy from a baby.'

'I realise that you've been living on pub rubbish for a while,' Esther observed critically as she looked over Jack's shoulder at how many potatoes he was peeling, 'but don't you think you might be overdoing your demonstration of your cooking skills? And did you *really* have to buy six lamb chops? We'll be living on mince until next week, so don't complain.'

'I wanted to make it a celebration feast,' Jack replied guiltily, 'and I was thinking of stepping down the street for a bottle of wine.'

'Well don't,' Esther pouted. 'I have to make the housekeeping money stretch whenever you take it into your head to play at being a chef. I did appreciate the breakfast in bed, believe me, but let's not get carried away.'

'It's not every day I get told I'm going to become a father again,' Jack said, grinning, as he put down the knife and folded her in his arms, 'so just let me celebrate in my own way.' He nuzzled her nose with his.

'Now who's this, for Heaven's sake?' Someone had knocked on the front door and Esther smoothed her hands down her apron as she walked down the hall and opened it. Jack gritted his teeth, crossed his fingers and waited.

'Uncle Percy!' Esther exclaimed as she leaned forward, pecked him on the cheek and stood back to let him in. 'To what do we owe this pleasure? Or is it business?'

'I don't normally conduct police business with a bottle in my hand,' Percy replied as he held up a large bottle of something red with a cork in the top.

'Hello, Uncle,' Jack said with a smile as he joined them in the hallway, 'you're just in time for supper, if you'd care to join us. Would lamb chops appeal to you after your recent meat pie diet?'

An hour later, as they sat around the dining table, Esther put down her fork and turned to Percy. 'This unexpected visit isn't a social one, is it?'

'How do you mean?' Percy replied with his best disingenuous smile.

'You're just back from wherever you and Jack were for the past few days and you probably haven't even been home to Aunt Beattie yet. You're armed with a bottle of wine — which is delicious, by the way — and Jack cooked far too much supper for the two of us, almost as if he was expecting you. What are you two up to?'

Jack's glance fell down to the table and Percy felt obliged to fill the ominous silence. 'How would you like to assist the Metropolitan Police again?'

'The last two times nearly got me killed,' Esther replied acidly. 'What do you want me to do this time — jump in front of a bus to test how fast the driver can pull on the reins?'

'Nothing like that, honestly — I couldn't bear to expose you to anything dangerous,' Jack began, only to be struck dumb by the furious look on Esther's face.

'So you *were* in on this plan, were you? I might have known. Married less than two years, a second child on the way and you want to use me as bait for an axe murderer or something?'

Percy raised an enquiring eyebrow in Jack's direction and Jack nodded. 'Due next Summer sometime.'

'Congratulations!' Percy enthused. 'You're hoping for a boy this time, I gather?'

'He'll get nothing at all if I'm lying up a back alley somewhere with my guts hanging out!' Esther objected as she began to rise to her feet.

Percy, seated at the end of the table, but close enough, put a restraining hand on her arm and reassured her. 'We merely wish you to do some book-keeping.'

'For Dick Turpin? Or Blackbeard the Pirate perhaps?' Esther protested, shaking off Percy's retraining hand, but making no further effort to leave the table.

'For an art dealer in Hatton Garden,' Jack replied reassuringly.

Esther sat down again, then looked quizzically back at Percy. 'Fraud?'

Percy shook his head. 'Jack can seek to sweeten the pill if he wishes, but I have too much regard for your intelligence. We believe he may have murdered his sister. However, there's no reason to believe that you'd be in any danger from him — we simply wish you to observe his movements and his manner, and perhaps acquire a photograph of him that we can show to witnesses.'

'Tell me more,' Esther said reluctantly, 'not that I'm saying yes, mind, but you've no idea how boring it is sitting here day after day nursing a whining infant.'

Her face screwed up in distaste as Percy and Jack between them recounted the known facts surrounding the death of Marianne Ormonde in a railway tunnel in Wiltshire and how it might be connected to her being pregnant to her own brother — the Edgar Ormonde that they wished her to seek a position with. They also impressed upon her that they almost had enough evidence to put him away, but needed the final pieces that would connect him to the circumstances leading to Marianne's death, and, in particular, confirmatory evidence that the child she'd been carrying had been his, and that therefore he had a motive to do away with her when she declined to have an abortion in order to avert any possible scandal.

'I don't know anything about art,' she objected.

Jack smiled again. 'You won't need to — that's *his* speciality. He and the other woman who works for him, a Miss Prendergast, who does his cataloguing and helps with the sales. Marianne — the deceased — simply kept the books of account and that's all he'll need you for. Books of account are books of account, whether they're for art galleries, garment manufactures, trade unions, butchers' shops or coalmines.'

'I have an infant to look after' was her next attempted excuse.

'And you've only just finished telling us how boring that is,' Jack reminded her. 'Mrs Bridges can come in every day and look after Lily. And before you say that we can't afford it, remember that you'd be paid a wage as a book-keeper for all the time you'd be working, and it's only a few streets away.'

'I'm breast-feeding, Alice is over sixty years old, and her youngest is a married woman in her twenties.'

'You can get a device that takes the milk from your breasts in advance, so that you can heat it up later,' Jack explained. 'Lucy uses one now that she's on her third, or at least that's what Mother told me. And it's high time that we tried to get Lily on something more solid.'

'I'm pregnant' was Esther's last throw of the dice.

'That's even better,' Percy responded with a smile. 'A real bonus, as it turns out, since we believe that the deceased was visiting a quack abortionist in Devonshire Street.'

'You're surely not suggesting that I sign up for an abortion?' Esther demanded, red in the face. 'If you recall, that was my excuse for getting all friendly with Pearly Poll, who tried to slit my throat.'

'Of course not,' Jack reassured her. 'But this quack will clearly wish to examine you when you call at his clinic seeking an abortion, claiming that Marianne Ormonde recommended him.'

'And that's all?' Esther asked, beginning to waver somewhat.

'That's all, believe us,' Percy replied consolingly. 'And it has to be more demanding than lying around the house all day.'

'Is *that* what you think?' Esther bristled. 'Any time either of you would like to change places with me for the day, nursing an infant, cleaning the house, shopping for food and cooking meals, just let me know, and I'll swap with you for a day or two strutting the streets looking for burglars and deviants.'

'Or nailing a man who shoved his own sister off a train?' Percy interjected. 'I think you just volunteered, my dear.'

Esther's mouth opened and shut several times before she broke into a giggle when she heard Lily's first plaintiff cry from the nursery.

'You have a deal. We'll just exchange duties, shall we? Jack, take Uncle Percy into the next room and give him his first lesson in nappy-changing.'

Chapter Eight

'It's highly irregular,' Chief Inspector Wallace objected as Jack and Percy eagerly explained their plan to him, seeking both his approval and his assistance. 'We don't employ women anywhere in the Met. for very obvious reasons.'

'That's why we sometimes lose out in our investigations,' Percy reminded him. 'It's all very well dressing some of our prettier young constables in cloaks and bonnets and sending them out in the half light down ill-frequented pathways, but we've got no-one with accounts experience who could pass as an educated young lady in the bright light of an art salon. She'd be in no danger at all, she can report back to Constable Enright on a nightly basis, and she'd be ideally placed to get the last remaining pieces of evidence we need to crack a case that Wiltshire wouldn't have had a prayer of solving without us.'

'Can you categorically assure me that she'd be in absolutely no danger?' Wallace asked.

Jack nodded vigorously. 'It's my wife we're talking about sir. The mother of my child, with another one on the way. I wouldn't let her within an inch of this caper if I thought she'd be exposed to the slightest danger.'

'She *was* the one who enabled us to put Jack the Ripper out of business, after all,' Percy reminded him. 'Then she was instrumental in drawing out of the woodwork a very nasty burglar and his homicidal sister. She's more than capable of looking after herself.'

Wallace made a pretence of examining his pipe bowl as he gave the matter deep thought. Eventually he looked up and nodded. 'Very well, but I don't wish this to be taken as any sort of precedent for the future, understand? However, it just so happens that we have an exchange programme operating at present with the New York Police Department, who're over here swapping ideas and studying our methods. We'll do this my way and I'll need a day or two to set it up. Come back here at four this afternoon — I'll have somebody waiting to meet you.'

The following Monday, just as the mighty bell of St Andrews in Holborn was announcing to the commercial fraternity that it was eleven am, a stocky gentleman in gaudy tweeds, with a ridiculously vulgar drooping moustache and incongruous brown boots rose to meet Edgar Ormonde and hand him his business card, while the smartly dressed dark-haired girl who'd been occupying the seat next to him remained where she was, as if indifferent to what was going on while she sat staring at the paintings on the wall behind the glass counter.

'Morgan T. Jacobs the Third and mighty grateful that you could find the time in your busy schedule to see me, sir,' the man enthused, while Ormonde looked down at him slightly disdainfully through his monocle.

'You wish to buy a painting or two?' he asked, as if doubtful of the gauche man's artistic inclinations.

'No, sir, I do not. Instead, I wish to put a business proposition to you.'

'You have paintings to sell, perhaps?'

'Those, and much more besides, although it is indeed the matter of paintings that brings me here to your fine emporium. I am fortunate indeed to be the heir to my grandfather, the original Morgan Timothy Jacobs, of whom you will no doubt have heard.'

'I can't say I have,' Ormonde replied haughtily.

'That is, if I may say so, doubly unfortunate, since among his business papers on his untimely death was a set of instructions to his heirs and successors, which contained within it a mighty testament to your reputation in the art world across the Pond. This is why I am seeking your assistance in the matter of acquiring masters on commission.'

Ormonde's expression softened somewhat as he gestured for his visitor to resume his seat, drew another chair alongside his and ordered Miss Prendergast to serve them all coffee.

'You have an art gallery in New York?' Ormonde said and Jacobs broke into a smile.

'More than an art gallery, depend upon it, sir. The finest house of *objets d'art* in Lower Manhatten, to which we wish to add the merchandising of the finest paintings from Europe, most notably those of the French Impressionists, for the dealing in which you enjoy a fine reputation. It would be our intention to acquire these through you and we would deem it both an honour and a privilege if you would deign to accept a ten per cent commission on all such acquisitions, to be added to your bill of sale upon shipment.'

'I'm sure we could accommodate you in that regard,' Ormonde smirked back, already calculating the potential for 'skimming' by inflating purchase costs. 'When would you wish to commence?'

Jacobs raised his hand to indicate that there was more. 'I have one more proposal to put to you, sir, if you would permit me. The fine young lady at my side is not merely here in order to brighten our morning with her beauty. She is, in truth, my niece Esther, daughter of my brother Solomon, who is currently serving his country in the United States Navy and who entrusted his daughter's education to your fine boarding school system, before she graduated and went to stay with a family friend in Bloomsbury. It is our ultimate intention that she should work alongside us in New York, when Solomon is discharged of his commission and takes up his rightful place as my business partner. However, in order to do that she will require a proper introduction to the world of art commerce accounting. We could, of course, put her through one of your English training colleges, but you would no doubt agree with me that they are inclined to be somewhat vulgar and to attract entirely the wrong sort of student. At the same time, dear Esther has led a sheltered life thus far, and would benefit considerably from experience in the matter of managing her own finances. In short, my brother and I would be mightily obliged if you could find her some paid work here in your fine establishment, preferably such as would acquaint her with the practice of financial accounting in the context of art transactions.'

Ormonde smiled unpleasantly across at Miss Prendergast, then turned to look down at Esther with an appraising smile. 'By a fortunate coincidence, Miss Prendergast has recently demonstrated that the keeping of books of account is not quite to her liking, so it would be of considerable assistance to me if your delightful and beautiful niece could commence work in that capacity with the minimum of delay. Shall we say tomorrow, at nine o'clock sharp, and at fifteen shillings a week?'

Esther forced a smile of gratitude to her face as her make-believe uncle slapped his thigh in delight and shook Ormonde's hand enthusiastically.

'Splendid! I'm most grateful to you, sir and I have no doubt that this will prove to be only the beginning of a fine and mutually profitable relationship between our two business houses. I'll have my people draw up the agreement and it shall be with you by the end of the month! Come, my dear,' he said to Esther as he took her elbow, raised her from her seat and escorted her proudly out of the front door that Ormonde held open for them.

'Thank you very much for that, Charlie,' Esther whispered as they walked back towards Clerkenwell.

'It was a pleasure, Ma'am,' Officer Charles Zolinskie assured her. 'But good luck working for that slimy critter.'

While Esther was securing her entree into Ormonde's art gallery, Uncle Percy was causing considerable apprehension to Michael Parsons back at Kemble Station. Monday evening was a quiet time and Parsons was humming quietly to himself, in anticipation of a pleasant night drinking tea and reading a book after taking over the ticket office from day shift porter Albert Bedser. But his smile froze as he walked into the booking hall and found Percy Enright sitting in a corner, wreathed in smoke from his battered pipe.

'Good evening, Mr Parsons,' Percy said quietly. 'May I have another word with you before you commence your duties for the night?'

'Certainly,' Parsons replied nervously. 'I need to take over from Albert behind the window there and we need to count the money at the end of his shift, so if you could just wait there until I call you through?'

'Certainly,' Percy replied, adding with soft sarcasm, 'I won't slope off to the Tavern.'

Parsons gave him the benefit of a wan smile and disappeared inside the ticket office. A few minutes later Albert Bedser left and Parsons appeared in the doorway.

'The pot's on — cup of tea?'

'Thank you, that would be nice,' Percy replied, smiling, as he followed Parsons through the door marked 'Railway Staff Only'.

'So what's this about?' Parsons enquired anxiously as he poured the boiling water into the teapot.

'I assume that you maintain a "lost property" service?' Percy asked.

Parsons nodded. 'Company policy — did you want to buy something cheap?'

Percy frowned. 'I'll ignore that, since presumably you're supposed to keep items until their owners claim them.'

'True,' Parsons conceded, 'but after three months we get to sell them. I can offer you any number of umbrellas or walking-sticks.'

'Where do you store them?'

'Over there in the corner, in those boxes.'

'And do you have any way of knowing which items were lost on any given date?'

'Not the exact date, no.'

Percy frowned. 'That's a pity, since I'm looking for something that would have been dropped, or left accidentally, on the night that you sloped off to the Tavern. Probably something small, but I can't be certain of that.'

Parsons eyes lit up. 'You mean that funny looking key?'

'I don't know *what* I mean exactly,' Percy admitted, 'but show me anyway.'

Parsons walked over to the far corner and from a cardboard container that had once contained railway brochures he extracted a gold-coloured key attached to a loop of string.

'Albert found this the following morning,' Parsons explained. 'He's the man you saw leaving just now — my opposite number on the day shift. It's part of the day shift duties to sweep out the front area, near the entrance door, because of all the leaves that blow in, particularly at this time of year. He told me he'd found it on the ground under the flower box that's got those dahlias in it. I remember because I've never seen a key like it and the string it's attached to is like the stuff my father uses to tie up his tomato plants. I guessed that it opens a garden shed or something, but no-one's ever claimed it.'

'The person who lost it had a very particular reason for not claiming it,' Percy muttered. 'May I borrow it for a day or so, if I give you a receipt?' Parsons looked uncertain, so Percy decided to play the constabulary card. 'Or would you prefer me to buy it off you, like all the other stuff you sell on the side?'

'If you put it like that, just give me the receipt,' Parsons mumbled, red in the face.

'Before I go, I have one more question for you,' Percy advised him.

'Ask away,' Parsons said invitingly, anxious to be rid of the man who could end his career with one letter.

'The night you closed up unofficially and went to your card game over the bridge there, did you leave the station lights on?'

'No, come to think of it,' Parsons admitted. 'I left the light on in this office, but I turned off the gas in the booking hall, to let people know that the station was closed. Why do you ask?'

'When you came back, it would have been dark in the station forecourt?'

'Black as pitch. But once I got back in, I re-lit the gas in the booking hall.'

'And there was no-one in the forecourt when you got back?'

'No-one that I saw. Nobody followed me in, anyway.'

'Thank you, Mr Parsons. You may enter into your records that this key was reclaimed. But I'd be grateful if you didn't mention who by.'

Chapter Nine

'This is Miss Prendergast, who you met during your first visit with your uncle,' Ormonde reminded Esther as he waved airily towards Abigail, seated behind the glass counter with the new catalogue lying face up on the baize cloth. 'She does the cataloguing and you'll obviously need to work closely with her as the items come in and out, since we record their purchase and sale values in a separate book for each, and the difference between them in the Profit and Loss Account book. Do you have any grounding in basic accounting techniques, Miss Jacobs?'

'Not really,' Esther replied with her eyes downcast and what was intended as an overawed expression on her face.

'That's not a problem — I'll soon teach you how I like things done here,' Ormonde reassured her as he indicated with a wave of his arm that she should accompany him through the double glass doors that led from the sales salon into the rear of the premises. Esther walked ahead of him, then stood politely in front of what appeared to be an office desk in the centre of the rear room. There was a kitchen of some sort to the side, with a gas geyser that presumably dispensed hot water and a sink that had three cups inverted on its steel surface, presumably left there to dry on a previous occasion.

'This is what I use as my office,' Ormonde explained. 'Obviously I spend most of my time in the sales room out there, but when we're quiet I can leave Miss Prendergast to mind the shop while I come back here to organise my schedule of auctions and exhibitions. As you can see, we also have refreshment facilities here and during the middle of the day you can sit with Miss Prendergast at that table in the corner and eat whatever you've brought for your lunch, although Miss Prendergast often takes her lunch break outdoors. Feel free to make yourself tea whenever you feel the need, but leave the coffee alone. It's imported and only I drink it. Any questions thus far?'

'I don't think so,' Esther mumbled in her most humble tone, giving silent thanks for the fact that life had not required her to earn her living in this fashion.

'Very well, then — upstairs,' Ormonde instructed her, gesturing towards a flight that led up behind a curtain that had been drawn to one side.

'I beg your pardon?' Esther said in a feigned tone of alarm.

Ormond smiled knowingly and suddenly Esther's feeling of alarm was genuine.

'Don't be concerned, Miss Jacobs, or may I call you "Esther"? The accounts are kept upstairs in my late sister's old room, where she maintained her work desk. Follow me up and I'll show you.'

He led the way up the stairs and Esther followed dutifully behind. At the top was a broad landing, leading to a large room on the right that appeared to be directly above the salon and a smaller one to the left that presumably looked out over whatever lay to the back of the premises. Ormonde gestured to the right, observed 'my living quarters', then held out his other arm invitingly as he added, 'You will be based in there.'

Esther deduced that she was intended to go the left, so she did. She found herself in what could best be described as a *boudoir* that still smelt faintly of what must have been the late sister's chosen perfume. There were mirrored wardrobes on either side of the room and a large bed under the window, with its foot pointing back out into the room. She was confused until she turned round and there, on the back wall, was a set of bookshelves that looked down on a chair with a matching desk, on which was an inkstand and a container of nib pens.

'My late sister preferred to work in her room,' Ormonde advised Esther with what threatened to turn into a leer as he gestured with his arm but kept his eyes on Esther's bosom. 'If you find it convenient we can maintain that arrangement and you may of course rest on the bed should you feel the need from time to time. The view from the window leaves a lot to be desired, but you will note that the usual facilities are located in the rear yard, which is accessed by the door on the left in my downstairs office. Go and sit at the desk and I'll explain how the books are organised.'

Glad to be safely seated, Esther paid dutiful attention as, one by one, Ormonde lifted down the ledgers, opened them and explained how he required items to be entered. In order to do so, he was required to lean over Esther's shoulder and she did her best not to grimace as she caught the smell of stale cigar smoke, and worse, on his breath. Having been through them all and with the volumes replaced on the shelves, Ormonde took delight in setting Esther imaginary tests.

'Let's see how well you've grasped the system,' he suggested. 'Assume that I purchased a Renoir from the Regency Gallery Auction for five hundred pounds. Where would you enter the sale price?'

Suppressing a bored sigh, Esther reached up to the shelf and took down the 'Acquisitions' book and looked at him enquiringly. 'You'd have to spell the artist's name,' she advised him in her best humble voice and Ormonde smiled.

'Excellent, my dear,' he replied patronisingly. 'Now, if I were to sell it for eight hundred?'

Esther pointed up at the 'Sales' book and Ormonde smiled condescendingly.

'You seem to have got it so far. Now, in this imaginary exercise I have made a notional profit of three hundred pounds. Where should that be recorded? This time, lift the book down.'

She did as requested, laid the book on the desk and opened it at the latest page.

Ormonde clapped his hands in an excess of appreciation and leaned forward eagerly, brushing closely up alongside her as he did so.

'And, as you can see,' he continued, 'the last entry was two days ago, recording a profit of two hundred and eighty pounds. Clearly, your next entry would be here.' He bent over beside her and pointed to the next available blank line on the ledger, as he announced, 'I'll go and get my draft notes on the next few entries that will be required.'

Esther sat down heavily at the desk, hoping that she had imagined the hand brushing her bottom as he moved away.

Early on Tuesday morning Percy instructed Josh Babbage to turn the coach and wait for him at the farm gate, then walked across the lawn towards the stables and coach house above which Bert Gregson had his accommodation. Bert was grooming the horse that normally pulled the coach and looked up as he saw Percy approaching.

'What d'yer want this time?' Bert enquired grumpily.

Percy tried the diplomatic approach. 'I believe I'm in a position to return some lost property, Mr Gregson.'

'Whaddyer mean?'

Percy extracted the key and string from his pocket and held it up in front of him. 'Unless I'm very much mistaken, this is your missing back door key. I noticed on my earlier visit that the back door was fitted with one of those new "Yale" type locks and this particular key may well have once been hung on the hook at the side of the back door to the farmhouse, using the sort of string favoured by market gardeners.'

'There's one way ter find out, in't there?' Bert replied gruffly as he put down the horse comb and led the way to the rear of the farmhouse. He used his own key to gain access, then put the knob in the 'snib' position, before taking the key from Percy and using it to release the lock again.

'Looks like yer right,' he conceded. 'Where d'yer find this?'

Percy was well prepared for this question and smiled as he lied, 'On the lawn there, just as I was walking up to see you.'

Bert's face darkened as he replied, 'I'm not a stupid yokel, Mr Whatever-yer-name-is, an' as yer can see, that lawn were scythed not two days since. I'd 'ave seen that key if it'd bin there, so where d'yer *really* find it?'

Percy was both embarrassed and chastened. 'Sorry,' he replied, 'I didn't mean to insult your intelligence, but I'm not at liberty to disclose where I found it. Police business, I'm afraid.'

'Yer found it near poor Miss Marianne's body, din't yer?' Bert asked accusingly.

'What makes you think that?' Percy enquired. 'You're wrong, as it happens, but what made you suggest such a thing?'

'Come this way,' Bert insisted with a jerk of the head, as he led Percy through the stables, up a flight of wooden stairs on the far inside wall and into a long straight room that contained an unmade bed, a table, two chairs and a wardrobe, as well as a wood stove in the corner.

'It ain't much, but it keeps me warm an' dry,' Bert advised him. 'It also gives me a good view o' what's goin' on yonder,' he added as he nodded towards the window.

Percy walked over and looked out; from that window Bert had a commanding view of the back door to the farm house.

'I couldn't say much last time I talked ter yer,' Bert explained, 'since Clarice were listenin' an' I didn't wan' ter be 'eard talkin' ill o' the master. The truth is that I seen both of 'em leavin' the 'ouse by the back door the night what Miss Marianne were found dead.'

'Were they leaving together?'

'No. Miss Marianne went first — stormed out like there was a ragin' bull chasin' er. She went chargin' off down the drive towards the front gate, dressed just like she 'ad been when I picked 'er up from the station earlier that evenin'. Then maybe ten minutes later I 'eard the door slam shut again, an' I looked out an' there were the master, in the act o' testin' the door ter make sure it were locked. Then I think I saw 'im stuff the key in 'is pocket, although it were dark o' course, so I can't be sure, but that's what it looked like.'

'How was he dressed?'

'Again, just like the mistress, the same clothes 'e'd bin wearin' when 'e arrived. That fancy bloody 'untin' jacket, 'is travellin' cloak an' that stupid 'at 'e's so fond o' stickin' on is 'ead. I think they call 'em "deerstalkers", although 'e's no better than all them other town folk when it comes ter shootin' — couldn't 'it a barn door at twenny paces.'

Percy smiled at the illusion and kept going while the man was in the mood. 'You told me last time I was here that when he got back much later you were obliged to let him back into the house because he claimed to have forgotten the key.'

'Yeah, that's right, but like I said then, it didn't look like 'e'd just bin ter the lavvie across the yard.'

'Describe how he was dressed then,' Percy requested.

Bert screwed his face up. 'Like a bloody scarecrow, 'e were. 'E'd obviously lost 'is stupid 'at somewhere, 'e were all red an' sweaty, like 'e'd done a day's harvestin', an' 'is 'untin' jacket were all ripped down one side. I reckon it 'ad a couple o' them fancy buttons missin' an' all.'

'What sort of fancy buttons?'

'Like they make outer deer's antlers, or somethin' like that.'

'Ivory?'

'Is that what it's called? Some sorta bone, anyway.'

'Would you prepared to sign a statement confirming all this, if I have one drawn up for you?' Percy enquired.

'I s'pose so,' Bert grumbled, 'since I were always brought up ter tell the truth. Mind you, it'll likely cost me me job 'ere, if the master finds out about it.'

'Let me assure you, Mr Gregson that if I get to make proper use of your statement, your master will be in no position to dismiss you — or anyone else employed here.'

Satisfied with his morning's work, Percy asked to be driven back to Kemble Police Station, where he once again sorted through the deceased's belongings. It was too much to hope that he'd find any bone buttons trapped in the late Marianne Ormonde's clothing, but on a whim he removed the scarf that had been used to gag her, in the belief that someone at the farm could identify it as having belonged to the unfortunate lady. Then he went back out to the front desk, where Constable Jacks advised him that Sergeant Oakley wanted to speak to him.

Thirty minutes later he was seated in the back parlour of a terraced cottage in Station Road, having been introduced to Martha Longhurst by a clearly disapproving Sergeant Oakley.

'Is it right that yer one o' they Scotland yard types what's lookin' inter that woman what got 'erself murdered in the tunnel?' Martha enquired.

'That's correct,' Percy confirmed, wondering what he might conceivably learn to his advantage from a lady described to him by the sergeant during their short walk down the road as the most unrepentant prostitute in the small township. 'She's got a bit o' competition these days and she's a bit past 'er prime,' Oakley had advised him. 'However, she can sometimes place us in possession o' useful titbits of information and she's very anxious ter avoid a charge that's 'angin' over her 'ead at present. She robbed an out o' town mark of a gold watch and she's lookin' at a two year stretch unless she can redeem 'erself.'

'Well, it's like this,' Martha insisted as she leaned forward to emphasise her point with a clear view down her ample cleavage. 'That bloke what they reckon's 'er brother were tryin' ter talk me inter tellin' anyone what was interested that 'e'd bin 'ere wi' me from ten o'clock 'til midnight that night they found 'er body.'

'Did he offer you money?' Percy enquired.

'No — 'e *give* me money,' Martha replied. 'Two quid, but I spent it already.'

'And did you promise to give him that alibi?'

'Yer what?'

'Did you agree to say that he'd been with you for those two hours?'

'Yeah.'

'Well, do us all a favour and don't tell him that you've reported this to us,' Percy advised her. 'That way you can keep your two quid, but if the matter comes to court, we'll need you to tell the truth.'

'Yeah, all right. What about the misunderstanding about the gold watch?' she asked Oakley, who smiled.

'We got it back and the gentleman yer stole it from is anxious to avoid it becomin' public knowledge how 'e come ter lose it, so we'll call it quits. But keep yer hands ter yerself in future.'

'Me gentlemen friends prefer it when I don't,' she grinned back.

'That alibi wouldn't have done him any good anyway,' Percy observed as they walked back up the road. 'He must realise that we'll know from Tom Savage that he was on his way back from Swindon during that time.'

'Maybe he's getting confused by all the detail,' Oakley suggested. 'I know I am.'

'How's Lily?' Esther asked eagerly as she pushed open the front door and threw her arms around Jack.

'Fine, so don't worry. Alice looked in as promised and between us we managed to get Lily to eat some mashed potato and carrot. Looks as if the milk counter can be closed until the next one needs it.

'You're sure she got enough to eat?'

'Take a listen — she's fast asleep, grunting with satisfaction. I offered Alice ten shillings a week, by the way, but she refused to take it. She said it was reward enough to have a "wee darling" to look after again.'

He was talking to Esther's back as she leaned over Lily's cot to reassure herself that nothing untoward had overcome her while her mother had been out in the wicked world.

'Are you going to get around to telling me how you got on during your first day working for Ormonde?' Jack enquired.

Esther straightened back up, turned and pulled a face.

'He's so *creepy* and I swear he deliberately touched my bottom when he was showing me over the books! How that poor Miss Prendergast puts up with him I'll never know. The room he's obliging me to work in is like some sort of religious shrine to his dead sister. Her photographs are all over the place, the room's been left exactly as it was — with her bed still in it, mark you! — and I wouldn't be surprised if her ghost's looking over my shoulder the whole time. Thank God it's only going to be temporary, that's all I can say!'

'Don't forget that the first thing we need is a photograph of Ormonde himself.'

'That shouldn't be difficult,' Esther pouted. 'The only photographs around the place that aren't just of the dead sister are also of him with her, the conceited oaf!'

'Will you be able to do the work?' Jack enquired solicitously and Esther hooted ironically.

'A child of seven could do the work, believe me! He went through it with me like he was some sort of ancient wizard revealing the secrets of eternal life, when in fact it's less complicated than managing our weekly bills. What I can't understand is why Miss Prendergast found it so difficult — honestly, you could train a child to do it.'

'Perhaps it was deliberate on her part,' Jack suggested, 'you know — pretending she couldn't do it so that she didn't have to. Or perhaps she's naturally stupid.'

'Perhaps,' Esther mused thoughtfully. 'But maybe it was to avoid being felt up by that dreadful deviant. I take it that I can't knee him in the privates if he does it again?'

'Not if you want him hanged for the murder of his sister, which you have to admit is a bit worse than a pain in the nuts.'

'So once I get you his photograph, can I hand in my notice?'

'That will depend on what Uncle Percy decides. And don't forget that you're going to have to make an appointment with that abortionist.'

Esther shuddered at the mere thought and put her arms around Jack. 'Hold me tight and remind me of how safe I am when you've got your arms around me. Edgar Ormonde's like a girl's worst nightmare.'

'Do you want me to prepare supper?'

'Later. Afterwards.'

'After what?'

'Take a guess.'

'I'm going to make tea,' Abigail Prendergast shouted up the stairs. 'Would you like some?'

'Yes please,' Esther shouted back, then placed her pen on the desk and negotiated the steep staircase down into the back room that served as both an office for Edgar Ormonde and a tea room for the two young women in his employ. Edgar himself was out at an art auction, so the two of them had the room to themselves.

Abigail made a slightly irritated noise as she looked into the biscuit tin, then closed its lid.

'We're out of biscuits again. I swear that Mr Ormonde eats them all when nobody's looking.'

'How do you get on with him?' Esther asked by way of polite conversation.

'He's alright, I suppose,' Abigail conceded, 'but watch his hands.'

'I've already encountered those,' Esther said grimacing. 'On my first day, what's more. Now I make sure that I never turn my back towards him.'

'He seems to like bottoms,' Abigail confided, 'but he only tried it once with me and I warned him that if he did it again I'd call in the constables. He pointed out that it would be my word against his and that I wouldn't find another place of employment in the London art world if I as much as breathed a rumour of accusation. These days I try to make sure that we're never in the same room together, but I was very glad when you arrived. Not that I want you to suffer it, of course, but at least now there are two of us, he may think twice before he lets his hands wander.'

'You must miss having his sister around,' Esther suggested and Abigail nodded.

'Mind you, not half as much as he seems to. At first, he seemed indifferent to her death, but in the past few days he's changed. Always looking up at that portrait of her in the main salon, and when you aren't here he spends a lot of time in the former bedroom where you're working. If you haven't realised yet, her clothes are still hanging in the wardrobe and her cosmetics are still on her bedside table. And some days I swear that her perfume fills the place. All very creepy, you must admit.'

'What was she like?'

Abigail thought for a moment, looked carefully towards the still open door into the salon, lowered her head and continued in a whisper. 'Very sweet, but very much under *his* thumb. She seemed scared to death of him most of the time and I think he did — well, *inappropriate* — things to her as well. It's one thing to fumble the backsides of female staff, which after all goes on inside the finest stately homes in the land when the lady of the manor isn't looking, but to do it to your own sister — ugh!'

'You mean he groped *her* as well?'

Abigail nodded with a sour expression.

'I came in here one day looking for more ink, and he had his hands round her — her *bosom*. Then there was one awful time when I came back early from my normal midday walk because it had begun raining and I didn't have my brolly and I heard — well, suggestive *noises* from upstairs. I made as much noise of my own as I dared, to let them know that I was back and I heard him curse loudly. Then a few minutes later he came down the stairs and ordered me to collect the Acquisitions ledger from the rear bedroom, where you work now. She was still in just her stays and the bed was all rumpled, like it had been slept in. She looked *so* embarrassed and ashamed and I'm sure he sent me up there just to humiliate *her*. Nothing was said, but it was obvious what I'd interrupted.'

'Horrible!' Esther confirmed with a genuine shudder.

'Embarrassing for me, as well,' Abigail confirmed. 'I couldn't look poor Miss Marianne in the face for a long while after that.'

They fell silent as they heard the front door to the salon open and Ormonde calling out, 'Why is there no-one at the counter? Miss Prendergast, get in here immediately!'

'Yes, Mr Ormonde,' Abigail replied dutifully as she rose quickly from the table and scuttled through the open glass doors. Esther gritted her teeth as she listened to Ormonde loudly berating Abigail and refusing to accept her explanation that she had been listening intently for the sound of potential clients entering the salon.

'Pig!' Esther muttered softly as she made her way back upstairs.

From behind her accounts desk she looked across at the photographs on proud display along the mirrored dressing table that Marianne must have used in order to beautify herself. Almost all of them seemed to feature both Marianne and her grubby brother and the only one Esther could see from that distance that was only of Edgar himself was one of a young boy in his early teens dressed in a sailor boy's outfit, no doubt an old family photograph that had survived from years ago, was now at least twenty years out of date, and would hardly do for the purposes that Jack and Percy had in mind. It would have to be one of the double photographs and the sooner she could acquire it, the sooner she could escape this awful place, where the continuing presence of the dead sister was almost palpable.

Her chance came two days later, on the Thursday of her first week of pretended employment, when Ormonde announced that he was travelling into Buckinghamshire to value some paintings that were being sold off as part of a family estate. Esther had, from the very start of her 'employment', travelled to and from work with her long-handled canvas shopping bag, into which she had sewn a secret compartment in the highest tradition of shoplifters everywhere and it was into this that she intended to slip whatever photograph she could find.

As she heard Abigail on the floor below explaining to a client that 'Mr Ormonde is away for the day, but he asked me to look out for you especially, and to show you our latest Morisot', she determined that the time was right. She moved across to the dressing table and looked carefully at her options. There was a large one of Ormonde and the lady who was presumably his sister, since many of the other photographs featured the same lady. It appeared to have been taken in a back garden somewhere and behind the two smiling people in the immediate foreground was some sort of two storied building that looked like a farmhouse.

Esther had been carefully briefed in her task and she turned the glass frame over carefully in her hand, then unhooked the sheet of cardboard that was holding the photograph in place. She sighed with satisfaction as she confirmed that there was another photograph beneath it, then removed the one she was about to purloin and carefully replaced the cardboard. As she placed the frame back carefully from where it had been sitting, lining it up as closely as possible with the clear dust-free mark on the lace dressing table cloth, she glanced down at what was now the new photograph on display. It was of a young lady — clearly Marianne herself — smiling at the camera as she sat on a seafront wall somewhere or other. Content with her acquisition, Esther heaved a sigh of relief and placed the photograph carefully in the hidden compartment of her shopping bag, making a point of leaving work slightly early, so as to avoid any premature return home by Ormonde.

Back at her own home, she proudly displayed the fruits of her theft and Jack smiled as he leaned down to kiss and congratulate her. Then he glanced down at the photograph.

'She doesn't look much like her painting in the gallery, but still a Hell of a lot more attractive than when I saw her last, on the mortician's slab like a side of beef in a butcher's shop.' He saw Esther go pale and hugged her to him. 'Sorry, my clever darling. Police work coarsens you, I'm afraid.'

'I tell you what,' Esther replied, 'I could never be a shoplifter. My heart was pounding like a steam engine while I was stealing it. I guess I must be naturally honest.'

'And naturally beautiful. Much prettier than this fancy lady, for all her wealth.'

'I don't think she had a particularly happy life,' Esther said sadly. 'But does she remind you of anyone?'

'No — who?'

'Lucy.'

'My sister?' He looked more carefully at the girl in the photograph and nodded slowly.

'Yeah, I see what you mean. But fortunately she's very much alive, with three children. Which reminds me — we're invited to the christening in a fortnight, in the church we were married in. Lucy's invited all her theatre friends, so it should be fun.'

Chapter Ten

'Have you removed a photograph from this dressing table?' Ormonde demanded furiously as he turned towards Esther, red-faced. Esther's heart leapt, but she managed to adopt an innocent and slightly offended look, as she replied.

'Most certainly not. Why would I have occasion to?'

'This dressing table and all that belongs on it, remain the property of my late sister, do you understand?' Ormonde bellowed back at her. 'Touch anything on here and you'll court instant dismissal, whoever your uncle is. Be in no doubt on that score!'

'Of course,' Esther replied meekly, suppressing the intense desire to demand to know who he thought he was talking to. His face remained an unhealthy red as he stormed from the back bedroom and thumped heavily down the stairs, allowing Esther to breathe more freely as she resumed her boring work.

An hour later she heard Abigail gently calling up the staircase that the morning tea was ready and that Ormonde had gone for what he had described as 'a long walk to calm myself'.

'I heard him bellowing at you earlier,' Abigail confided. 'What did you do wrong?'

'Nothing,' Esther insisted. 'He seemed to be of the belief that I'd removed a photograph from the dressing table that he keeps in that creepy shrine of his that he insists that I work in. It's really a strain on my nerves, being up there, surrounded by a dead woman's belongings — some days I could swear that she's glaring up at me from that ominous bed that fills half the room, as if she was laid out ready for her funeral.'

Abigail shuddered slightly. 'You'd be as well not to talk in such terms to Mr Ormonde,' she warned Esther. 'He's inclined to believe in all that nonsense about the spirits of the dead returning to trouble us and on one occasion he went so far as to mention his beliefs to me. It was shortly after Miss Marianne died — not a week later, as I recall — and he told me that he'd visited one of those women who defraud the more credulous of society out of money in return for placing them in so-called communication with the souls of those who have passed over. The charlatan had apparently advised him that Miss Marianne's spirit is restless and remains — "earthbound" I believe was the expression he employed — because of the tragic way in which she'd died.'

'How *did* she die, exactly?' Esther asked with the appropriate degree of innocence, hoping to learn what explanation Ormonde was giving to those around him.

'She threw herself from a train while the balance of her mind was disturbed,' Abigail advised her, 'or at least that's what Mr Ormonde says.'

'Was that the coroner's opinion?'

Abigail shook her head. 'There's been no coronial enquiry as yet, because — or so I believe — the police are investigating the circumstances surrounding Miss Marianne's untimely end. There was a young gentleman here from Scotland Yard, enquiring of Mr Ormonde when he last saw his sister and under what circumstances. The accident occurred down in Wiltshire, where Mr Ormonde has a residence to which he and his sister would resort at weekends.'

'And did this police officer give you any reason to believe that Mr Ormonde might have known more about his sister's death than he was admitting?'

'Certainly not,' Abigail replied stiffly. 'Mind you, the young man was most agreeable to the eye and I hope he continues his enquiries here. I met him in the street shortly before you arrived here and he gave me cause to believe that he might be seeking my further acquaintance.'

Esther suppressed a smirk as she imagined Jack weaving his boyish charm and she tried to return the conversation to something more profitable, if only to obviate the need for Jack to once again turn on the charm in the direction of a young art assistant who was quite comely in an old-fashioned looking way.

'And Mr Ormonde believes that the spirit of his dead sister may still be wandering loose here in the house, given her untimely end? Is it not suggested by these "Spiritualists" that those who die by their own hand are condemned to remain earthbound until their originally allotted span of life here in this world has expired?'

'You clearly know more about these things than you were originally prepared to admit,' Abigail replied with a slightly suspicious look as she collected the tea cups and headed for the hot water geyser. 'As for Mr Ormonde, he seems to have become a changed man since Miss Marianne died. He was so confident before then — totally possessed of his own belief in his infallibility. Since then, he's been more prone to sudden outbursts, as if his nervous system's in disarray. I do hope he's not sensing the spirit of Miss Marianne here in the building — if so, he might encourage her to show herself. I'd simple die if I saw her ghost and I couldn't for the life of me bring myself to work upstairs in her old room, the way you're called upon to do.'

'Don't worry,' Esther replied, grinning mischievously, 'if I see her wraith emerging from the wardrobe, I'll be sure to scream and let you know.'

'Don't talk like that, even in jest,' Abigail shuddered as she walked back out into the salon, leaving Esther deep in thought.

'I have to submit my report to the Assistant Commissioner by the end of the week,' Chief Inspector Wallace advised Percy as he pierced him with one of the stares for which he was so famous. 'It had better be good, since it's costing us so much. And when can we expect your nephew to resume his duties?'

'He's having to help look after the child while his wife performs her valuable role inside the suspect's business,' Percy reminded him, 'and it would be a shame to forfeit that wonderful work done by our American colleague.'

'So have we got enough evidence to buckle this man Ormonde?' Wallace enquired, provoking a thoughtful shake of the head from Percy.

'Not quite, sir, although the circumstantial case is building nicely. We're pretty sure that we can prove that Ormonde — or at least, a man closely resembling him — boarded the same railway carriage as the deceased, just as the train was pulling out of Kemble Station. A man answering a similar description got off the train at the next stop — Swindon — and hired a cab back to Kemble. Later today I hope to be able to secure a photograph of Ormonde obtained for us by Esther Enright, my nephew's wife, in the hope that the cabman from Swindon can identify him as the man who needed to return to Kemble so late at night.'

'So where did he go when he got back to Kemble?'

'He paid a local carrier to take him back to the converted farmhouse that he owns in a nearby village, where he and the deceased had spent the weekend, but not before he'd been seen searching for something he may have dropped at the station entrance in his pursuit of his sister shortly before she met her death. We believe that "something" to have been the key to the back door to the house they'd both left earlier, and one of the servants employed at that house — the coachman and gardener — can confirm that Ormonde had earlier left the house in pursuit of the deceased and that when he returned later that night, he tried to pass off his presence at the back door, minus the key, as a mere visit to the outside lavatory, although the key was by then missing from its usual place behind the back door. Finally, we have the evidence of a local tottie that Ormonde bribed her to give him an alibi for the hours between ten and midnight that night.'

Wallace nodded as he took in all this information. 'I can agree with you that the circumstantial case is a good one, but do we have nothing that directly links him with the woman's death?'

'We may have, sir, although no guarantees. According to the man Gregson — he's the coachman I mentioned a moment ago — when Ormonde turned up back at the house, his jacket was ripped and had several buttons missing from it. These were presumably all the result of his struggle with his sister as he heaved her out of the carriage, and the missing buttons were quite distinctive, made out of ivory or something similar. I'm planning on going to the Lost Property Office at Paddington, in the hope that some cleaner found them when the carriage was being turned round in London. If so, and we can match them to the torn jacket, then we can link him directly with some sort of scuffle.'

'Is that all?' Wallace demanded. 'And you haven't mentioned any motive for his murdering his sister. A jury will need a good motive, as you well know.'

'That's pretty strong, sir. We can put together a fairly persuasive collection of bits and pieces to suggest that the deceased was carrying her brother's child. We can prove that they had some sort of argument on the evening she died, suggestive of her having cancelled an appointment with an abortionist here in London, much to his annoyance.'

'Is that your motive?' Wallace enquired with a further frown. 'Surely she could have given birth and been forced or bribed to keep quiet about who the father was? That sort of thing happens so frequently these days that it's hardly a disgrace any more, although God knows it should be!'

'Perhaps not a disgrace in Whitechapel, Mile End or Putney, sir — but in the sort of fashionable circles in which Ormonde lives and conducts his art business? Even if she'd kept quiet about who the father was, the mere fact that she'd conceived a child out of wedlock would be disgrace enough for a man as conscious of his social image as our Mr Ormonde.'

'So has this wife of young Enright managed to unearth anything of additional value?'

'Early days yet, sir. I'm planning on speaking with her later today and finding out what she's managed to learn so far, but her presence there is as much a matter of keeping the suspect under observation as anything else.'

'And how much is this costing us in baby-minding fees?'

'Nothing at all, sir. Mrs Enright has secured the services of a near neighbour who's prepared to do the work for less money than Ormonde's paying for unwittingly clasping our viper to his bosom.'

'So why does Constable Enright need to remain off active duties?'

'His wife's peace of mind, mainly. I recommend that we continue to go along with that arrangement, sir, at least until we can be certain that there's nothing more to be gained by having our own spy in the enemy camp. As an added bonus, it just so happens that Esther Enright's expecting again, so we can also use her to investigate the possibility that Ormonde's reason for killing his sister was her refusal to go through with the abortion. Among the items we found in her purse was the address of a shady clinic in Marylebone, so if our suspicions are correct, we can also nab ourselves a quack abortionist. That alone, I feel sure, would afford Her Majesty great satisfaction.'

'Very well,' Wallace relied grumpily. 'I'll report upstairs that we have a strong circumstantial case out of all the work you've done thus far, but you'd better think of some way of getting us the sort of "smoking gun" stuff that impresses juries, if we're going to see Ormonde swing.'

Jack and Percy entered what looked like a massive jumble sale in the largest church hall imaginable, as the Lost Property Senior Clerk proudly explained to them how the various compartments within the network of shelves were labelled with the dates, stations of origin and type of train.

'Take this one fer example, sirs,' he invited them as he pointed proudly at a section close to the double entrance doors through which they had just passed. 'That's the 0735 from Bristol to London Paddington and each of the sections bears the date o' the service, like that one there. It musta bin rainin' in Bristol that mornin', seein' as 'ow there's so many umbrellas in that cubby 'ole. Now, if yer just gives me the name o' the service, an' the date, we'll see what we've got fer yer, shall we?'

Percy consulted his notebook and gave the Clerk the details. He led them proudly down between two lines of shelves, muttering to himself as he announced the various service sections they were passing. After what felt like a hundred yards further down, towards the back of the room, he stopped at a vertical line labelled 'Cheltenham to Paddington', then selected '9.15pm' from the descending line and rummaged through a pile of boxes until he turned with a triumphant smile and handed them a medium sized cardboard box.

'There yer go, gents. If it's something bulky, like a 'brolly or summat, there'll be a piece o' paper in there, tellin' yer which number it's stored under in a separate section at the end there. But as yer can see, it were a quiet night, wi' just somebody's 'at an' a bag full o' cachous or summat like that. The paper bag belongs ter the company, an' it's only what yer finds inside that's "lost property".'

Percy smiled and reached in the box for the deerstalker hat, which he handed to Jack. 'Anybody we know?'

Jack looked inside the rim of the hat and smiled. 'It was lost by someone called "G. Ormonde", according to this carefully sewn-in name label.'

'I think we might know someone of that name,' Percy said, grinning. 'At least it puts him on the train, but of even more direct significance are what this good man called "cachous". Look at these and be pleasantly surprised.' He reached into the paper bag and extracted three ivory jacket buttons, two of which still had material attached to them, suggesting that they had been torn from the garment on which they had originally been sewn.

'So?' Jack asked.

Percy tapped his nose to indicate that the matter was not for discussion in the presence of a lost property clerk, then turned to their guide through this Aladdin's cave. 'Thank you, Mr Jenkins, you've been most helpful, and of considerable assistance to Scotland Yard in its investigation of a most foul murder.'

'Glad to 'ave bin of 'elp, gents,' Jenkins replied as he proudly puffed out his chest. 'Would it be in order fer me ter tell the missus?'

'Indeed it would,' Percy replied, 'and thank you again for your invaluable assistance.'

Back inside the coach, as it left the forecourt of Paddington Station, Jack was curious.

'Did those buttons belong to Ormonde?'

Percy nodded as he reached inside his jacket for his pipe and tobacco pouch, and began to organise a celebratory smoke. 'They did indeed. According to the man Gregson — you remember him, the coachman-cum-gardener? — when Ormonde got back late that Friday evening his jacket was torn and appeared to be missing a few buttons. I'd bet Bermondsey to a brick that somewhere in his wardrobe at home is a jacket showing signs of recent repair and possibly a new set of buttons.'

'You're not about to suggest that Esther goes searching in his wardrobe, I hope?'

'Indeed not, but at least we know what to look for if we have occasion to apply for a search warrant.'

'And if we don't?' Jack enquired.

'I'll think of something,' Percy assured him. 'And now we'd both better think of something to explain your absence from father duty when we get you home.'

'How *could* you just walk out and leave Lily like that?' Esther demanded the minute that Jack and Percy appeared through the front door. She had her hands on her hips, which was normally not a good sign.

Jack moved towards her, intent on giving her a hug, but she stepped backwards and turned a baleful eye on Percy.

'You! I might have known! Whenever Jack runs off the rails, there's usually an Uncle Percy explanation. So what excuse have you both cooked up *this* time?'

'Jack's blameless,' Percy explained with his best smile. 'I called shortly after lunchtime and ordered him back on duty. Between us we've found some more evidence against your current employer.'

'All very glib,' Esther replied, far from mollified, 'but Mrs Bridges was a little nervous about being left alone like that. Supposing Lily had taken a bad turn or something? What sort of father walks out of the house, leaving his child in the care of a neighbour?'

'Half the fathers in London, in my experience,' Percy replied with a knowing smile, 'but I take it that dear little Lily came to no harm?'

'No, as it happens, but no thanks to you two. I just hope that the experience doesn't cause Mrs Bridges to back out of our arrangement. And there's nothing organised for supper, since that was supposed to be Jack's job. How are you at peeling potatoes, Uncle Percy?'

'Well experienced, as it happens,' Percy smirked back, sensing that the storm was subsiding, 'but I'm even better at buying portions of stew from cook shops. From memory you have one just round the corner in Aldersgate, so supper's on Scotland Yard, and Jack can peel the potatoes while I'm gone.'

'So, in the confident belief that your employer Mr Ormonde hasn't dictated a full confession to you while handing you invoices, what have you managed to learn so far?' Percy asked as they dug heartily into their lamb stew an hour or so later.

'You mean apart from the fact that he's an arrogant, overbearing, selfish, unfeeling pig?' Esther replied, still not yet quite pacified.

Jack chuckled. 'I could have told you that for myself. As for his assistant...'

'Yes?' Esther glowered back at him across the table. 'Miss Prendergast took some time to tell me that a charming young man came to visit them and accosted her in the street a few days later, and how she's hoping that he wants to become better acquainted with her.'

'It's thanks to my undoubted charms that we got you into the business in the first place,' Jack reminded her, at which she bristled even more.

'No it wasn't — it was that lovely American gentleman who posed as my uncle. He was quite handsome himself and he most certainly didn't lead my husband astray, like *some* uncles of my acquaintance,' she added with a scowl at Percy, who was not prepared to be deflected from the task in hand.

'You haven't even begun to answer my question, my dear.'

'Don't you "my dear" me, Uncle Percy,' Esther retorted as she put down her fork in what threatened to be an impromptu hunger strike. 'Every minute I spend in the so-called employ of that insufferable prig makes my flesh crawl. Not to mention the ever-lingering feeling that the dear departed Marianne Ormonde hasn't fully departed yet.'

'How do you mean?' Jack enquired, his face reflecting his sudden alarm.

'Well,' Esther continued, 'apart from the fact that the room I'm required to work in is her former bedroom and everything's all laid out as if she was about to walk back in, there's still the lingering smell of her perfume, which she must have applied with a fire hose. Then there's his obsession with the belief that her spirit lingers around the place. And he's very particular about keeping everything the way it was — he noticed that missing photograph the following day and all but accused me of stealing it.'

'Well you did,' Jack reminded her untactfully.

'Don't remind me!' she replied heatedly. 'I hope you don't want me to steal anything else.'

'No,' Percy replied quietly, 'but I might be asking you to take something back.'

'I beg your pardon?' Esther demanded and Percy reached into the attaché case he'd been carrying when he first arrived and extracted the deerstalker hat and jacket buttons, along with what looked like a lady's scarf, which was all creased and crumpled.

'Would I be correct in deducing, from what you said a moment ago,' he enquired, 'that Ormonde has an unhealthy obsession with the prospect of his dead sister coming back to haunt him, in the tradition of the worst type of "penny dreadful" broadsheet?'

'Apparently,' Esther confirmed. 'According to his assistant Abigail Predergast, he's been consulting one of those "medium" types and he's now of the firm belief that his sister's spirit can't rest because of "the tragic way she departed this life", to use the phrase adopted by the old fraud he went to visit.'

'Interesting,' Percy observed quietly. 'So, if things started to appear in that room you're working in — things that are connected with "the tragic way she departed this life", to use the appropriate phrase — do you think it might unsettle him a little?'

'A *little*?' Esther echoed. 'From what I can tell, it would be likely to drive him insane!'

'Enough for him to confess to what he did in your hearing, do you think?'

'Steady on, Uncle Percy,' Jack cautioned him, which Percy ignored.

'It's a standard technique we employ at the Yard — you get your suspect so thoroughly rattled that he either confesses on the spot, just to ease the pressure on his brain, or he says something in an unguarded moment that gives him away.'

'So what are you suggesting?' Esther asked, far from enjoying the recent change of topic. 'That I organise some sort of séance or something?'

'In a way, I suppose,' Percy replied with a growing smile as his brain began working overtime. 'These objects here on the table are all associated with that night when Ormonde pushed his sister out of the railway carriage. If they were to appear silently in that room...'

'I'm a book-keeper, not a conjurer,' Esther objected, as Percy raised his hand for silence and continued as if she hadn't interrupted.

'You can organise that, since you work in that room and presumably there are times when you're in there on your own?'

'Most of the time,' Esther confirmed,

Percy's smile grew wider. 'We might start with the hat,' he mused. 'Ormonde lost this during the struggle in the carriage, or so it would seem. Whatever the cause of its loss, it was during that last fateful trip with the deceased. So if it appears out of the blue, somewhere in the room where you work?'

'He'd probably have a heart attack,' Esther confirmed, her mouth set in a determined grimace. 'Then you could arrest me for causing his death.'

'She has a point, Uncle Percy...' Jack began, only to be silenced by a man who was more interested in being a Detective Sergeant than an uncle.

'Nonsense!' Percy insisted. 'A man like that doesn't have a heart. And should he die of shock, that would be the result of his own guilty conscience. You would simply be confronting him with what he's done — like we do in all police interrogations.'

'I'm not a police officer,' Esther objected. 'And he's bound to accuse me of planting the hat in there, behind his back.'

'Which you will of course firmly deny, with an air of outraged innocence,' Percy advised her.

'Is that before or after I expire out of sheer terror?' Esther demanded.

'The more unsettled you appear yourself, the more it will convince Ormonde that you had nothing to do with it.'

'I'm really not sure I'm up to this, in my delicate condition,' Esther objected.

'Talking of which,' Percy reminded her, 'don't forget to visit that abortionist.'

'The offhand way in which Jack treats his first child,' she retorted, 'I might be better having a *real* one, to prevent our second being abandoned whenever he hears the call of duty.'

'That's settled, then,' Percy insisted. 'Start with the hat and I'll start on the washing up.'

Long after Percy had left, Esther sat morosely at the kitchen table, staring at the wall. Jack tried everything in his power to lighten her mood, but nothing seemed to work.

'You don't know what you're both asking,' she said out loud eventually and Jack took the seat next to her and reached for her hand.

'It was Uncle Percy who asked,' he reminded her. 'For myself I wouldn't have dreamed of such a terrible strategy. But it can't result in any danger to you, can it?'

'You don't know what he's like,' Esther reminded him. 'At the best of times it's like working on the edge of a volcano. Even Abigail Prendergast's scared to death of him and she's been there a lot longer than me. If I do what Percy asks and start to crank up the pressure in his mind, he could go completely berserk.'

'Or he could simply crumple up and cry, and perhaps confess it all,' Jack suggested.

'Fat chance!' Esther insisted. 'Like I said, you don't know the man. And you don't have to be there to witness his darker moods. He really is *very* scary, even at the best of times.'

'Imagine what it must have been like, being his sister,' Jack reminded her and her face screwed up in distaste.

'You're both assuming that she got pregnant to him by consent. I wouldn't be surprised if it was *rape*.'

'Don't you think you owe it to her to expose him?' Jack suggested. 'You could take a weapon to work with you, just in case.'

'Like what? How long do you think he'd continue to employ me if he saw a kitchen knife poking out of my shopping bag? Or a billy club down my blouse?'

'Good point. To be perfectly honest, I don't think you should expose yourself to such risks anyway. You're not a police officer in the first place and you're only a woman after all.'

'*Only* a woman?' Esther bridled. 'What exactly did you mean by that?'

'Well, I mean...' Jack offered, pleased that she'd taken the bait.

'What you mean, Jack Enright, is that women are weaker than men. In body maybe, but not in the head. We aren't all put on this earth simply to open our legs to get pregnant and then open them again to give birth.'

'I didn't mean...'

'Didn't mean *what*, precisely? That I'm not capable of doing underhand police work, simply because I'm a woman?'

'Undercover police work,' Jack replied pompously, knowing precisely which buttons to press.

'Underhand police work, in this case. Well, let me remind you that you're talking to the woman who exposed the Ripper, when all you men were blundering around Whitechapel looking stupid. The woman who confronted a mad slasher of prostitutes who was all set to slit her throat. The woman who...'

'The woman who I love,' Jack murmured as he gathered her in her arms at the precise moment when she needed it and held on to her as she burst out crying.

'I'm terrified of what you're asking, Jack,' she burbled, 'but I'll be damned if I let you write me off as a mere woman! That's what got poor Miss Ormonde killed and it'll be a woman who sees to it that she gets her revenge!'

'I believe you,' Jack said reassuringly as he pressed her even closer and smiled over her shoulder at his realisation that Uncle Percy wasn't the only one who knew something about human psychology.

Chapter Eleven

The determination to prove Jack wrong about women that had led to Esther's initial outburst had slowly dissipated over the weekend that followed, to the extent that as she walked through the front door of Ormonde's art gallery on the Monday morning, she was hard put to conceal the trembling hands and the tightness of chest that affected her normal breathing pattern. The deerstalker hat concealed beneath the pack of sandwiches she had brought for her lunch was burning a hole in both her shopping bag and her courage. She felt sure that it must be obvious to anyone who took a cursory look beneath the lunch that she knew she would not be able to bring herself to eat, such was her nervousness at what she had foolishly undertaken to do.

The only bright light on her horizon lay almost a week away, when she would travel to Barking in order to see her latest niece baptised into the Church of England. That was, of course, assuming that she could survive Ormonde's fury when he discovered the ridiculous looking hat on the dressing table in the same room that Esther was expected to sit working on her accounts, awaiting the predictable outburst from the employer of whom he was already little short of terrified. She prayed to God for the courage to see it through, but in the event it was the victim of her intended subterfuge who made it possible by his own action.

She'd spent the first quarter of her working day staring at the columns of figures in her Profit and Loss Ledger Book while her mind tortured itself with the enormity of what she was planning, when Ormonde came up the stairs carrying a small white envelope. She smiled weakly as he came into the room and he smiled back.

'I must apologise profusely for not having given you your wages on Friday, my dear. I'm sure that, given your family's undoubted wealth, you were in no urgent need of fifteen shillings and my only excuse is that I'd grown accustomed to having only one employee, but here it is anyway.'

'Thank you,' Esther replied with appropriate gratitude in her voice, then froze in indignant disbelief as Ormonde placed the envelope down on the desk immediately beneath her left arm where it was extended across the ledger page, gazing at her bosom for a lingering moment before turning abruptly and walking out of the room and down the stairs.

A few moments later she heard Ormonde down in the salon, engaged in his usual smarmy sales routine with a customer, and the time would never be more right. She swiftly extracted the deerstalker hat from its place of concealment and scuttled over to the dressing table. Placing the hat carefully in the centre, where it couldn't possibly be missed, she grimaced in satisfaction and went downstairs to offer to make the morning tea.

'Coffee for you as usual, sir?' she asked breezily as Ormonde came through to the back with a self-satisfied smirk, a bill of exchange in his hand.

'Yes please,' he beamed, 'and this morning we can all enjoy a custard cream with our morning tea, because I just sold that Pelez — the circus scene. I'll just go up and leave this bill on your desk, Miss Jacobs, and once you've recorded it, place it in the banking envelope, so that I can walk it down the street when I go to lunch.'

He took the stairs two at a time and Esther stood with her back to the room, taking as long as she could with the hot water, tea and coffee grounds as she braced herself for a yell of outrage from upstairs. Instead it fell deathly quiet until she heard Ormonde descending the stairs slowly and turned in time to see him return into the back room, ashen-faced, holding the deerstalker in front of him at arm's length, as if it were an unexploded bomb or a dead cat. Without a further word to either of his employees he opened the back door and stepped out into the rear yard like a man walking in his sleep.

'He doesn't look very well,' Abigail observed unnecessarily during the ensuing silence. 'Is he heading for the lavatory?'

Esther leaned forward and looked through the still open door. She continued to watch as Ormonde disappeared inside the storage shed located along the back wall and re-merged with a container of restorer liquid, which he poured all over the hat before throwing it on the ground and setting fire to it.

'What's he doing?' Abigail asked in a hoarse stage whisper.

'Setting fire to his hat,' Esther chortled quietly.

A small blow for Marianne, she thought. *And I've only just started.*

'I don't have an appointment, I'm afraid,' Esther explained to the starchy-looking middle-aged lady in the nurse's uniform who was guarding the front desk, 'but Dr. Weinberg was recommended by a friend and I'm on my lunch break from work.'

'That's all right, my dear,' the nurse reassured her. 'The doctor doesn't have anyone with him at present, so I'll just nip into his consulting room and enquire whether or not he can see you on spec.'

A few minutes later, Esther was seated in front of Dr Weinberg's long desk, preparing to conduct her second deception of the day as she looked across as pathetically as she was capable, wringing her hands nervously in her lap as she surveyed the sleek aquiline features of the man in his mid forties with a stethoscope draped across the lapels of his white coat and an encouraging smile on his thin lips.

'What can I do for you, Mrs Jacobs?'

'Miss Jacobs.'

'My question remains.'

'I'm pregnant.'

'Most women who consult me *are*. Do you wish me to supervise your ongoing pregnancy and final delivery?'

'You may not have got my drift,' Esther replied. 'I'm *Miss* Jacobs.'

'And why should your lack of marital status be of significance to your physical state?'

'I don't want to be pregnant,' Esther replied in what she hoped was a suitable tone of desperation.

'And what makes you think I can assist in that ambition?'

'You were recommended by a good friend of mine — Marianne Ormonde. She intended to accompany me in person by way of introduction, but unfortunately she died a few weeks ago.'

'And in what way did this Miss Ormonde suggest I might be able to assist you?'

'I think we understand each other, Doctor,' Esther insisted in a slightly more determined tone. 'The only remaining question will be the size of your fee.'

'I need to examine you first,' Dr Weinberg replied. 'How far gone are you?'

'Three months, so far as I can tell. I've missed two monthlies and I've been experiencing morning sickness.'

'Very well, go behind that screen and take off your outer dress and all your underclothes below the waist. Then lie on the table in there and call me when you're ready. I'll get Nurse Frobisher in here while you're getting undressed.'

Fifteen minutes later, Esther was grateful that she hadn't attempted this subterfuge without being pregnant and equally grateful for the professional opinion that the child was sitting correctly in her womb and was probably about the size and shape of a bean. The doctor sounded reassuring about the baby's general health, so her journey had been of value to her, as well as to two Scotland Yard detectives who would soon be in a position to take an unethical doctor out of circulation.

'You are indeed near the end of your first trimester, Miss Jacobs, and if I understand the reason for your referral by your friend, you don't wish to progress to your second. Would I be correct?'

'Yes.'

The doctor studied her face for a moment before changing the subject. 'From your facial features, and of course your name, would I be correct in believing that we share the same Semitic ancestry?'

'I'm Jewish certainly — what of it?' Esther demanded defiantly.

'Did you consult your rabbi before coming to visit me?'

'Why should I? I'm not Orthodox and the rabbi isn't the father of the child. The only person I consulted was the father and I need to know how much, since he'll be paying.'

'Thirty guineas, plus two days in my clinic next door at a further ten guineas a day, so fifty guineas in total. Payable in advance, of course.'

'Of course,' Esther confirmed, with a facial expression that combined relief with gratitude. 'When can it be done?'

'Nurse Frobisher can make the appointment, so see her on your way out.'

'Thank God I was never placed in the same position as those poor girls who really need to get rid of their disgrace,' Esther said as she hugged Jack tightly in the hallway. 'I felt so *guilty* and even though the doctor seemed nice enough it all felt so dirty. Will he go to prison for a long time?'

'A few years anyway,' Jack informed her, 'but the real hardship will be that he'll be struck off, which means that he'll never be able to practice medicine again. Not legitimately, anyway. But tell me about Ormonde's reaction to the hat.'

Esther took great delight in describing Ormonde's almost catatonic state when confronted by the deerstalker left on the dressing table and she was able to go through it all again an hour later when the knock on the outside door heralded the arrival of Uncle Percy with a delicious smelling paper parcel.

'I stopped off at Farringdon Markets on the way back from Paddington. It's fish with fried potatoes, and if you turn the oven on to keep them warm, we can have them for tea.'

'I'm just back from Swindon,' Percy announced over their mutual murmurs of contentment regarding the new delicacy that he had brought with him, although the smell was beginning to overpower the kitchen and Esther had insisted on opening a window, 'and I'm delighted to be able to report that the cab driver there identified Ormonde from that photograph that Esther got for us. And thanks to her undoubted courage in rattling him with that hat of his, we've obviously had a good week. Plus, as an added bonus, we can consign Dr Weinberg to the labour queue. What did he say about Marianne Ormonde?'

'As soon as I mentioned that she'd been the one to recommend him, he seemed to know that I was after an abortion,' Esther advised them, 'so I think we can conclude that she was too. And Ormonde's just the sort of filthy deviant to have been responsible — if he ogles my body one more time, I can't guarantee that I won't shove a hatpin into where it'll hurt most.'

'Wouldn't you prefer to go on torturing his mind?' Percy asked with a worried frown.

'But each time I do that we'll be losing the evidence against him, surely?' Esther queried. 'He burned the hat that proved he'd been on the train.'

'But that's *all* it proved,' Percy reminded her, 'and we have other evidence to prove that, so don't worry about losing that hat. The same's true for the jacket buttons, so try him with those next.'

As Esther's face fell at the mere prospect, Jack came to her defence. 'She's only just recovering from the business with the hat, Uncle. Remind us again why it's so important to play these mind games with him.'

Percy sighed and put down his fork. 'We convince him that his dead sister's come back to haunt him, so that when we pull him in for questioning he's in such a weakened mental state that he'll be relieved it's all over. He may even plead with us to stop the sister seeking her revenge. He wouldn't be the first to seek police protection in exchange for coming clean on what he's been up to.'

'But protection from a *ghost*?' Esther argued. 'Have you ever known *that* before?'

'Believe me,' Percy assured her with a grimace, 'the threat posed by a ghost is nothing compared with the prospect of being done to death horribly by former members of a gang that you've just peached on.'

'You mean "no", in other words?' Esther insisted. 'But if you can prove that Ormonde was on the train when Marianne died, why can't you just arrest him now, without all this play-acting about ghosts and suchlike?'

'Because,' Percy explained with another long sigh, 'he'll just pretend that she committed suicide by jumping out of the carriage before he could stop her.'

'He's left it a bit late to pull that one, surely?' Jack pointed out.

Percy nodded. 'To trained and experienced police minds like ours, yes. But never under-estimate the stupidity of your average jury, given that the man's rich enough to employ the best legal brains in his defence. In the hands of someone like Charlie Gill or Marshall Hall, his silence becomes the shocked response of a grieving brother who somehow felt responsible for his sister's suicide when, like the God-fearing man that he is, he wouldn't condone her having an abortion after she fell pregnant to a local boy in Kemble.'

'You should have been a lawyer yourself, Uncle Percy,' Esther said appreciatively.

'I value my soul too much,' Percy replied with a sneer, 'but you get the general idea?'

'Yes, but do I *really* have to pull a stunt with the jacket buttons?' Esther replied with a pouty face. 'And so soon after the subterfuge with the hat?'

'Yes, and no,' Percy replied as he stared at the wall, deep in thought. 'Yes, you *do* have to, but no, we'll leave it for a day or two, to let him think that his dear dead sister was just playing a single prank on him. If we give him time to regain his composure, the shock will hit him even harder.'

'Even though he's a piece of disgusting slime, I almost feel sorry for him,' Esther replied sadly. 'If we manage to bring him in, will he hang?'

'Most certainly,' Percy replied, 'but take it from an old detective dog, never — *ever* — start feeling sorry for your suspect. Just remember what he did to his sister.'

'I'm beginning to think that he did more to her than just push her off a moving train,' Esther replied as her face set in revulsion. 'I don't think their sexual antics were entirely voluntary on her part. It's sickening!'

'Keep those thoughts uppermost in your mind,' Percy advised her. 'And never forget that we're doing all this for her.'

'I'm not likely to, while I can still get the whiff of her perfume in the room I'm obliged to work in,' Esther muttered.

Percy looked up sharply. 'Can you still smell it?'

'Did I not just say so?'

'Do you know what perfume it is?'

'No, but there are several large bottles, all with the same label, on the dressing table in the room. I can soon read the labels, why?'

'Because the housekeeper at the country retreat near Kemble mentioned the lingering quality of the deceased's perfume. "Tuberose" wasn't it, Jack?'

'I can't remember the precise name of it,' Jack admitted, 'but I remember the housekeeper complaining that Marianne's room reeked of it. But, as Esther asked, why might that be important?'

'We might add ghostly smells to ghostly reappearances of objects connected with the death,' Percy replied with a malicious grin.

'I hope you won't expect me to dress up as the deceased and leap out of the wardrobe or something?' Esther replied jokingly. Or, at least, she hoped it would be taken as a joke.

'I can't imagine anyone who looks less like Marianne Ormonde that you,' Jack reminded her reassuringly, in case

Esther had unwittingly supplied Percy with another fiendish idea. 'And you were the one who suggested that she looked a bit like Lucy.'

'Yes, she did, come to think of it,' Percy muttered. He took the photograph from the inside pocket of his jacket and studied it closely. 'With her hair down differently, and perhaps dusted a little, so that it isn't so strikingly fair as Lucy's...'

'I do hope I haven't dropped your sister in for something horrible,' Esther murmured as her head rested on Jack's chest later that night. 'I won't be able to look her in the face at the christening if Uncle Percy gets her involved in all this as well.'

'He'll stop at nothing to get his man,' Jack muttered ominously. 'Nothing.'

'Have you noticed anything odd about Mr Ormonde's behaviour in the past few days, or is it just me?' Abigail Prendergast asked as she poured the morning tea in the back room.

'How do you mean?' Esther replied, she hoped innocently.

'Well, first of all there was that weird business with him setting fire to his hat, then he asked me while you were out on Friday if I'd heard or seen anything unusual in that back room that you work in, and then this morning he was *very* abrupt with me.'

'In what way?'

'Well, I came in early, to complete the preparation of the new catalogue that he's taken down to the auctioneer, and he came in carrying an overnight bag, and I merely asked, by way of polite conversation, if he'd spent the weekend at his country place in Wiltshire. He just about exploded on the spot, asked me what business it was of mine and told me to spend more time on my duties than speculating on where he'd spent the weekend. I'm a bit concerned that he might be suffering some sort of mental strain. Is the business secure financially? Only I really need my job here.'

'Trust me, Abigail, the business is going from strength to strength, to judge by the Profit and Loss Account. But perhaps he's got some personal concerns — like with a lady friend or something.'

Abigail sniggered. 'I don't think I've ever heard him mention a young lady, although — well, I think I told you what I suspected with his sister. But apart from her, I've never known him show any interest in another woman.'

'Apart from us, you mean,' Esther reminded her with a look of distaste.

'Only once, with me. But what about you, cut off up there in that horrible bedroom?'

'A couple of times, but I'll be ready with my hatpin next time. But where do you think Ormonde had been, if not down at his country retreat?'

'No idea,' Abigail admitted, 'although I know he has a club up in the West End where he often takes clients for lunch. I believe that those gentlemen's clubs have bedrooms as well. Perhaps he stayed there, but he was most insistent that he hadn't been down to Wiltshire. In fact, come to think of it, he's never mentioned the place since Miss Marianne died. He's never made any reference to her either, not since that lovely police constable was here that day.'

'Perhaps he's in mourning for her,' Esther suggested. 'From what I can tell, her bedroom's just the way she left it.'

'I couldn't do what you're doing,' Abigail advised her with a shudder. 'Work in a bedroom left by a dead woman, almost as if she'd just gone down the street for a few minutes.'

'You mentioned one other time that you'd never been to their country place — were you ever invited to?'

Abigail shook her head. 'No, I rather got the impression that it was their "special" place. You know, him and his sister?'

Just then they heard the front door opening and Ormonde's voice calling out. Abigail went red in the face, placed her tea cup hastily down on the table and raced through into the salon.

'Sorry, Mr Ormonde!' Esther heard her say. 'I was keeping an ear open for the door bell, honestly! It's just that Esther made some tea and we were just talking about boyfriends.'

'Perfectly normal, for two attractive young ladies like yourselves,' Ormonde replied, 'and I really must apologise for my outburst this morning, when I first came in. I spent last night at my club and I'm afraid that I didn't sleep too well, so please forgive me.'

'Of course,' Abigail replied, as Esther came through to join them and offered to make some coffee for their employer. He accepted the offer with a smile and followed Esther into the back room, where she kept her distance while her back was turned at the sink, not wishing to invite any unwanted hands around her person.

'Have you ever been to an art auction?' Ormonde asked.

'No, I haven't, but I suppose I might need to learn something about them if I'm to be of value in New York,' she replied casually.

Ormonde smiled invitingly as he offered to extend her introduction to the art world. 'There's an auction this coming Thursday, at the Regency Gallery in Bond Street. I've got a few Impressionists in there and copies of our complete catalogue will be available for those attending. Perhaps you might like to accompany me and deal with any potential interest?'

'I'd be delighted,' Esther assured him with as much enthusiasm as she could coax into her voice. She handed over the coffee and was about to head back upstairs when Ormonde looked up from the table with an almost despairing look on his face.

'Are you happy working in that former bedroom of my late sister's?'

'Of course,' Esther replied. 'It's very peaceful, back there away from the street noise. Plus there's that lovely perfume that I can occasionally smell.'

'What do you mean?' Ormonde demanded sharply and Esther feigned surprise.

'Nothing in particular, sir. It's mainly when I first go in there in the morning and I can detect what must have been your sister's perfume. "Tuberose", wasn't it?'

'Yes, it was,' Ormonde advised her in a voice that was almost a croak. 'But you only notice it when you first go in, you say?'

'Mostly,' she advised him with her best innocent look, 'although there are times when it seems to grow in strength, almost as if someone was opening one of the bottles on the dressing table. I take it those were hers?'

'Yes, they were, but they are never opened, so I'm at a loss to understand how you could smell them more strongly in the middle of the day. Does anything else unusual ever occur while you're working in there?'

'Such as?'

'Anything. Noises, sudden changes in the air. Cold spots in the room. That sort of thing?'

'Definitely not, although if I take your meaning correctly I can say that I don't believe in ghosts.'

'I wish I could say the same,' Ormonde muttered to himself, then looked up sharply as he remembered that he had an audience. 'Very well, don't let me keep you from your work. And make a note for Thursday.'

The first three days of the week passed without further incident or unusual conversation and Esther made careful preparations for her next sleight of hand. She had the three very distinctive ivory buttons which, according to Percy and Jack, had come from Ormonde's jacket during his struggle with his sister in the railway carriage. They were safely tucked into the pocket of her own jacket as she waited patiently for Ormonde to venture out onto the street in order to hail a cab, and then slipped as silently as she could across the room, took the buttons from her pocket and left them precisely where she had placed the deerstalker hat on the previous Friday. Then she hastened down the stairs with what she hoped was an eager smile just as Ormonde announced that he had a cab waiting, and with a cheery farewell to Abigail, who gave her a jealous look, Esther stepped out into the street and climbed into the cab.

She spent two boring hours smiling enthusiastically at potential art buyers to whom she handed out Ormonde's brochures, then sat with her employer at the back of the sales room as two out of the five Impressionist paintings that he'd placed on sale went for well above their 'reserve' price. Ormonde took the opportunity to slide his hand up and down the material of her skirt as it lay smoothed against her thigh, making it seem that he was merely reading the auction list and she gritted her teeth and prayed for it to be over, consoling herself with the revenge that she would be exacting upon their return.

Eventually her ordeal was at an end and as she assured Ormonde during the return cab journey that she had found the auction experience 'most enlightening and helpful', she was almost gloating over what awaited them. The fear and apprehension that she'd experienced when planting the hat had not returned, but had been replaced with a cold desire for revenge on behalf of Marianne and all the other women that this disgusting wretch sitting across from her had taken advantage of.

When they got back to the salon it was close to lunchtime and Abigail took off for her usual walk while Esther unpacked her sandwiches and made herself another cup of tea, plus a cup of coffee for her employer, who sat gleefully playing with the two bankers' drafts that had secured the sales of the paintings. The unsold ones were due to be returned the following day and Ormonde also occupied his time amending the few remaining copies of the catalogue that they'd brought back with them.

Esther deduced that Ormonde was not planning on going out for any lunch, so she took as long as she could eating her sandwiches, drinking her tea, listening to Ormonde droning on about art auctions he had known, and praying for Abigail's return. Eventually Ormonde took a paper and pencil, scribbled down the details of the morning's sales and instructed Esther to make the necessary book entries after lunch. When she could delay her time downstairs no longer she made a slightly embarrassed excuse about needing to 'nip outside' and sat for as long as she dared on the outside lavatory before making her reluctant way back inside the salon. As she re-entered the back room she heard Ormonde on the final stair up to the next floor and his heavy footsteps as he walked into his own apartment, presumably to change.

As she waited with bated breath she heard him walk back across the upstairs landing, then — seemingly on a whim —

entering the back bedroom. There was a pause, then a yell of horror, following which Ormonde came down the stairs at a rate perilous to his safety, raced across the salon, flung open the front door, and hurled the coat buttons as hard as he could across the street, where they bounced off the front door of the diamond dealer's premises on the far side. Then he ran down the street as fast as he was able, looking behind him in abject terror every few yards, and eventually flagging down a passing cab.

Almost immediately afterwards, Abigail Prendergast returned from her lunchtime perambulation, wide-eyed as she looked behind her back out into the street. 'Did you see that?' she asked.

'I most certainly did,' Esther replied with a mischievous grin. 'You may be right about his mind being a little disturbed of late.'

Chapter Twelve

The small group hovered, cooing and smiling almost in homage, over the sleeping bundle in the shawl that seemed none the worse for having recently been sprinkled with water from the baptismal font, but was not noticeably any holier for having been received into the fellowship of God. But it was the grandmother, and hostess of the celebratory luncheon that had followed, who could not resist voicing her sentiment once again.

'This is how family christenings should be, Jackson. In the church in which you were christened, as well as Lucy. The church in which your late father and I were married, and in which you were joined in holy matrimony to Esther. There was no need to have Lillian baptised in some obscure church in that wicked city, almost as if you were ashamed to show her here in Essex.'

'Saint Andrew's Church in Holborn is hardly "some obscure church", Mother,' Jack argued, 'and you *were* there to see that for yourself. It's not as if we had our daughter smuggled out to the Jesuits or something.'

'Even so,' his mother insisted, 'there are protocols and traditions to be observed. Fortunately your sister seems to be aware of that; even though she actually lives within the parish of Holborn, she saw fit to honour the family tradition for the third time.'

'I need to feed her once she wakes up,' Lucy explained as she stepped away from the family group, leaving them nowhere to feast their eyes except on each other.

'And I need to rescue Lily from Aunt Beattie and Uncle Percy,' Esther whispered to Jack as she too exited the group. This left Jack with his mother and his brother-in-law Edward Wilton, the father of the recently christened Sarah Wilton, husband of Jack's sister Lucy, and a successful architect with an established practice operating out of premises in Chancery Lane in which the growing family also resided.

'So how's the detective work going?' Edward asked Jack, in order to break the silence.

Constance tutted in faint disapproval before offering her contribution. 'It's to be hoped that it provides him with enough income to support *his* growing family, like your profession does, Edward. Now that Esther is expecting her second, he'll hopefully shake off all this police nonsense and find himself a suitable position in the City. His father came to no harm there and as you can see from all that surrounds us, it can be the means to acquire a far better home than a few cramped rooms in Clerkenwell.'

'I'd better go and help Esther,' Jack offered as he slipped backwards out of the group, anxious to avoid yet another homily from his mother on his irresponsibility in following his Uncle Percy into the police force, a speech he knew by heart by now. He found Esther with Lucy, who still had a sleeping Sarah in her arms, while at her knee was her oldest, two year old George.

'Mother's off on her favourite topic,' Jack complained, 'so if anyone asks, I was needed over here, right?'

Lucy smiled one of her lighthouse beams at him. 'Thank you *so* much for taking the trouble to come along, both of you. It means so much to Teddy and I to have family around us on such an important day as this.'

'We seem to be somewhat outnumbered,' Jack commented as he cast his eyes round the room, which seemed to be dominated by 'colourful' types sporting striped blazers, yachting caps, cricket trousers, party dresses, and — in one case — full morning dress in imperial purple.

Lucy chuckled. 'They are a bit overpowering, aren't they? But once I'd invited one, I simply had to include them all, and you know what theatrical types are like.'

'Where did you find them all?' Esther asked with an amused smile. Lucy and she were the greatest of friends, and it had been Lucy's foresight that had brought Jack and Esther back together when they were in danger of drifting apart a few terrible years back in the past. Lucy had also provided a sanctuary in her own home for Esther when she'd been forced to abandon her temporary residence following an arson attack by a serious disturbed woman out to kill her.

'They're all from the Holborn Players Theatre that I belong to these days,' Lucy advised them. 'You remember that I always had a hankering to go on the stage? Well, Mother wouldn't allow anything so vulgar, but once I was married I persuaded Teddy that there was no disgrace in belonging to an amateur company, and next month I'm playing Desdemona.'

Jack turned to smile at Esther. 'I'd better go and collect Lily, like you were pretending to do when you used the excuse to get away from Mother. If Uncle Percy drinks any more beer, he's likely to drop her, and he'll never hear the end of it from Aunt Beattie.'

Freed of the burden of child-minding, Percy drifted back to the buffet table, under stern marital instruction that he'd had enough beer for one afternoon. He was helping himself to a glass of lemon squash to wash down his third pork pie when he was accosted by an eager lady who gave the impression that she was about to bid for him at auction and wanted to examine her potential purchase more carefully before committing herself.

'You're that Scotland Yard chappie, aren't you? Uncle of that younger Scotland Yard chappie?'

'Guilty as charged, madam, but that now means that you have the advantage of me,' Percy returned as the beer rendered him more sociable than he might otherwise have been on this formal social occasion that was everything he most detested in life.

'Hilda Fancourt, lady of leisure, widow of this parish — well, the Parish of Holborn actually — and godmother to the child that is now committed to God, whether God approves or not.'

'Friend of the happy parents?'

'One of them, certainly. Lucy's my leading lady.'

'Oh yes, her theatrical hobby. Are you another actress?'

'I was once, until *anno domini* robbed me of any claim to thespian dignity. I now direct.'

'Traffic?' Percy joked, then wished he hadn't as the large lady pealed with laughter that shook her ample bosom like a sapling in a gale.

'No, *theatre*, you naughty boy, you. I'll be directing your niece in *Othello*, whose opening night is barely a month away. You simply *must* come along.'

'Theatre is all about illusion, isn't it? A bit like my profession, in a way.'

'Ah, but you people cannot create illusion on the same grand scale that we do in the theatre. From mountainous peaks to desert islands, and from royal palaces to humble graveyards. Only last year we put on a play about a king of Scotland who murdered his way to the throne, the name of which I won't mention for reasons of pure superstition. But for that we had to switch effortlessly from a "blasted heath" on the windswept Scottish moors to the royal palace of Glamis. And in between we had to materialise the ghost of the murdered former king.'

'You produced a *ghost*?' Percy asked in a tone of pure disbelief.

'Of course we did, oh ye of little faith. He appeared right on cue in the midst of the assembled company, not once, but twice.'

'You presumably don't employ mediums in the theatre?'

'Only the medium of fine prose professionally delivered by dedicated actors. Plus a few technical tricks of the trade.'

'You have people in your theatre who can produce ghosts?'

'One person, anyway. Frances Fordyce, our stage manager. She can also do thunderstorms, banshee shrieks, galloping horse hooves and ethereal lights.'

'Can she only do them in the theatre?' Percy enquired, an idea already forming in his mind.

'She's only required to produce them on stage, but she could generate them in the fish market, or inside St Pauls, if necessary.'

'So how does she do it?'

'Come along for yourself and find out. On Monday morning, as it transpires, we're having a meeting to discuss the set for *Othello*, so if you'd care to join us, I'm sure Frances could allay your lingering doubts. And don't pretend that you don't have any, because it's written all over your face. You may think that you present a "deadpan" to the world, but your eyebrows tell all. Should you ever wish to play the role of a malevolent persecutor, the part will be yours for the asking. The theatre's halfway down Bedford Row, on the right as you approach it from Theobald's Road. However, I see Jeremy is about to throw one of his wobblies when he's not got an audience for one of his risqué jokes, so *"a domani?"*, as the Italians have it.'

'Who was that talking marquee tent who accosted you?' Jack asked as he joined Percy at the table, to which he'd been sent by Esther in search of a second helping of sherry trifle.

'She was a bit on the large size, wasn't she?' Percy agreed. 'But she gave me a wonderful idea, if Lucy's up to the challenge.'

On the Monday morning Percy found himself in an alien world, as he walked uncertainly down the gentle slope between rows of seats in the stalls of the Holborn Players' Theatre towards where a group of enthusiasts were marking out portions of the stage with chalk lines and employing technical terms like 'masking' and 'stage left'. He stood there uncertainly for a moment, feeling a bit like a harlot in a vicarage, until his brief companion of two days previously spotted him and bellowed for his attendance on the stage.

He was required to go out through a side door and back in through something called the 'wings', and when he finally fought his way through the drawn back curtains, it was to discover that most of those who had been occupying the stage had taken a tea break. The only person left on stage alongside Hilda Fancourt was a slightly built woman who made Hilda seem even more enormous as she effected the introductions.

'Frances, allow me to present a gentleman from Scotland Yard whose name is so much a State secret that even I don't know it.'

The lady gripped Percy's hand as if she intended to remove it from the end of his arm as he revealed his true identity.

'Percy Enright, Detective Sergeant, investigating your ability to produce ghosts.'

'Percy's your greatest sceptic, Frances,' Hilda boomed and Frances bowed her head in acknowledgment as she opted to speak for herself.

'It's very simply done, actually. If you give me a moment, and if you'd care to go back out into the stalls, I'll re-appear as my own ghost at centre stage. I can't be there in the flesh at the same time, unfortunately. Even I have my limitations.'

Percy did as instructed, and a few moments later the heavy drape curtains swished shut across the front of the stage and furtive movements could be heard behind it. Then the house lights were extinguished, leaving the entire theatre in total darkness for several moments until the curtains re-opened and the echoing voice of the stage manager boomed out through some sort of megaphone device.

'You thought me dead, but I live again among you.'

A circle of light appeared centre stage and within it the grinning face of Frances Fordyce.

'Are you convinced, or do you wish me to grimace menacingly?' came the same ghostly voice. 'But once concede that I exist, the room shall be restored to lightness once more.'

'I'm convinced,' Percy shouted, 'but I need to see how it's done.'

'It's the simplest illusion in the book,' Frances explained as she reappeared on stage in the flesh a few moments after the lights had been restored. 'Also one of the oldest. Follow me into the wings and I'll show you.'

A bemused Percy went back on stage and followed the directions indicated by her voice, behind the curtains to the left of the stage, where a beaming Frances stood waiting to welcome him into her domain. Then to his utter amazement he also heard her voice behind him and he whipped round to see her also standing there. He looked back quickly at where he had first seen her and finally realised that he had been looking into a mirror which had somehow not contained his own reflection.

'Welcome to Pepper's Ghost,' Frances explained with a grin. 'Perfected some thirty years ago by the man after whom it was named, and the deception device that gave rise to our popular phrase "It's all done with mirrors". Every theatre in the world regularly employs some version of it or other, and you just saw the simplest.'

'So it's simply a mirror?' Percy said. 'But how did you get the image on-stage?'

'Another mirror which you couldn't see because it was a plain sheet of glass and the light shone brightly on it. The glass back here was simply tilted at an angle to reflect the image of me, and the one on stage was placed at a forty-five degree angle to it. Once a bright light is shone on the primary image in front of the first screen, it attracts and dominates the eye of the beholder of the screen on stage, whose fixation on the image causes them not to notice the second mirror.'

'So simple,' Percy muttered in admiration.

'Yes and no,' he was corrected by Hilda Fancourt, who had joined them in the wings to invite Percy to partake of tea and biscuits in the cast tea room behind the stage. 'It's imperative that nothing breaks the beam of light between the two mirrors, which requires careful stage direction. In that play I mentioned to you, when we produced the ghost of a dead king at a banquet, we had to ensure that not a single member of the cast playing the nobles at the banquet went in front of the table. That tended to produce a rather "wooden" effect until Frances had the brilliant idea of making the table deep as well as wide — almost square, in fact — so that we could put some of the main players down the side.'

'So you could reproduce this trick anywhere?' Percy asked as he dunked his second ginger biscuit into his tea.

Frances nodded. 'You just need two separate areas — preferably two single rooms — so that one can be brightly lit for the image to be transmitted, and the other in as much darkness as you can get away with, to project the image into it. In the play that Hilda mentioned, we had the actors at the banquet carrying torches in with them as they arrived, which they extinguished simultaneously when it was time for the ghost to appear. Then while the lead actor came to front of stage to express his horror for the benefit of the audience, one of the actors at the table deliberately stood in front of the second mirror while the stage lights were subtly increased over the course of the soliloquy.'

'Could it be done through a limited space, like a window?' Percy asked, his mind already thinking it through.

'Yes, it could,' Frances replied after a slight pause, 'but then you'd only get the head and shoulders. The rest of the body would be cut off, as it were, giving the impression that the upper half of the body was suspended in mid air.'

'Even more effective,' Percy murmured.

'For what exactly?' Hilda demanded. 'Do I detect that you have some need of our theatrical services in some police investigation?'

'If I did, would you be amenable?' Percy enquired eagerly, 'always assuming that a suitable donation was made to your theatre funds?'

'Now you speak my language again,' Hilda replied with a smile. 'When would you require us?'

'I don't know that I do, yet,' Percy replied cautiously, still deep in thought. 'Tell me, who does your actors' make-up?'

'The actors themselves, in the main,' Hilda replied. 'The more experienced of them learn make-up as part of their training.'

'Including my niece Lucy?'

'One of the best,' Hilda assured him and Percy reached into his jacket pocket for the photograph of Edgar and Marianne Ormonde.

'How easily do you think she could make herself resemble this lady in ghostly form?'

'The work of mere minutes,' was the encouraging reply from Hilda.

'If you wanted to blur the features a little,' Frances added helpfully, 'we could drape a fine muslin cloth over the first mirror, or Lucy could don a light veil. If you want cobwebs from the grave, we have a piece of very worn lace that does the job admirably.'

'Remember that we open with *Othello* in just over three weeks,' Hilda reminded him. 'Whatever you have in mind would need to be completed by then.'

'Believe me, it will,' Percy assured her. 'If we need to resort to that, of course,' he added.

Chapter Thirteen

'It's very good of you to keep feeding us like this, Uncle Percy,' Esther said as she smiled across the kitchen table, 'but we normally have to sing for our supper. I know you well enough to suspect that once again this isn't a social call. We saw you only two days ago at Sarah's christening, so what are you up to now?'

'Very astute,' Percy muttered as he reached into his pocket and produced a crumpled scarf of some sort.

Jack's eyes widened in apprehension. 'Uncle Percy...' he began in a warning voice, until silenced by a wave of Percy's hand.

'Esther's a big girl now and doesn't need to be shielded from the truth. In fact she's going to get even bigger in the weeks that lie ahead of us, so the sooner we use her to maximum effect in her role as Ormonde's book-keeper the better.'

'"Financial Controller", if you don't mind,' Esther reminded him with a smirk. 'But what's that on the table?'

'At the risk of putting you off these fine lamb chops,' he replied, 'it's the scarf that was used to gag Marianne Ormonde before she was pushed off the train. She was probably screaming at the time.'

'Charming!' Esther shuddered. 'But let me guess — you want this to appear miraculously on the dressing table in the sister's former bedroom?'

'So quick on the uptake,' Percy grinned back appreciatively. 'But perhaps with a heavy dose of the dear departed's perfume? You did say that there were large quantities of it in the room?'

'Yes, on the same dressing table, as it happens. But the other tricks we pulled on him didn't produce any confession, so what makes you think this will?'

'Because Jack and I will have visited the establishment earlier in the day, to ask some more penetrating questions and to crank up the pressure on the man.'

'We will?' Jack asked, just as Esther raised her hand in protest.

'So I'm required to keep a straight face when my husband appears at my place of employment, pretend that I don't know him from a bar of soap, and smile indulgently while he oozes charm all over Abigail Prendergast, is that it?'

'Precisely,' Percy confirmed.

'And then, for an encore, I place this horrible gag thing on the dressing table, having soaked it in the deceased's perfume, then sit back and listen carefully to his confession?'

'You're a quick learner,' Percy complimented her.

'I'm also not a fool, Uncle Percy. You don't know the man. He's very wobbly in the head already and when we hit him with this, he's likely to run out of the place screaming, and perhaps get run over by a carriage in the street.'

'That would make the need for a confession somewhat unnecessary,' Percy replied and it was Jack's turn to object.

'Quite apart from putting Esther under more needless stress when she's in a very delicate physical condition, if he does himself in without any confession we're going to have a lot of explaining to do to Chief Inspector Wallace. Is there no other way?'

'Can *you* think of one?'

'No, not right at this moment, but give me time.'

'Time is something we don't have,' Percy advised him. 'Esther's going to start *looking* pregnant before much longer and Lucy opens in her latest play in a few weeks' time.'

'Don't tell me you're planning on dragging Lucy into this as well?' Jack demanded disbelievingly. 'Mother would never forgive you.'

'Your mother needn't necessarily know,' Percy said, smiling. 'And she may not be required anyway. All we have to do at this stage is pick the day when we visit Ormonde in his lair — the day that Esther plants the scarf on the dressing table.'

Esther's old apprehensions returned with a vengeance as she approached the front door of the gallery on Wednesday morning, the tell-tale scarf almost calling to her from where it was hidden inside her shopping basket when she bid a cheery 'good morning' to Ormonde and Abigail as they stood together studying the latest catalogue on the glass counter. She went straight upstairs to her prison-like office in the bedroom and tried to occupy her attention with the almost laughingly small number of entries that she needed to make as she waited apprehensively for the sound of the front door bell, and the arrival of the two men from Scotland Yard.

Fortunately they delayed until morning tea was almost out of the way, then the doorbell chimed and Abigail looked out through the dividing doors and gave a giggle of delight.

'It's that nice young detective back again, but he's got an older man with him this time,' she whispered back at them.

Esther excused herself and hurried back upstairs, while Ormonde put on his best straight face and walked into the salon area to greet them.

'We've met before, have we not?' he enquired of Jack, who nodded.

'Indeed we have. I'm Detective Constable Jackson Enright of Scotland Yard and this gentleman with me is Detective Sergeant Enright.'

'Has Scotland Yard turned into a family business?' Enright replied sarcastically and Percy simply stared back at him before speaking in his most authoritative tone.

'Talking of family matters, we have a few more questions for you regarding the night of your sister's tragic death.'

'I believe I've told you all I can, Inspector.'

'Sergeant. And no you haven't.'

'Meaning?'

'Meaning that we have witnesses who can confirm that you were on the same train as your sister. The train from which she fell to her death.'

'Then your witnesses must be either lying or mistaken.'

'Including your own coachman?' Percy demanded sternly and Ormonde's face paled slightly. Percy pressed home his advantage. 'You originally told my constable here that the last thing you saw of your sister was when she retired to her room on the Friday evening — the evening of her death. But according to your coachman and handyman — a Mr Gregson — you followed her shortly after she left the house that evening, and were back at the house much later that night — the night, let me remind you, that Miss Ormonde finished up in the railway tunnel. So where *did* you go that evening, Mr Ormonde?'

For the first time their suspect looked flustered and remained silent until Percy threw another squib into the interrogation. 'If it assists your memory, Mr Ormonde, there's another coachman we've already had the advantage of speaking to. The one who brought you *back* from Swindon on the Friday evening, after you presumably alighted in a hurry from the same train that your sister fell from. Can you explain that?'

Ormonde began to resemble a cornered rat as he looked across at Abigail Prendergast, listening spellbound from behind the counter, and mentally vowing never to do anything so bad that it justified being questioned by this horrible ferrety-faced bully.

'Miss Prendergast,' Ormonde instructed her, 'this might be a good time to see if the printer's finished our new catalogue.'

'Yes, Mr Ormonde,' Abigail replied meekly as she collected her gloves and shopping bag from under the counter and slipped out through the front door, taking a few deep breaths of relief. Whatever her employer had been up to, she still needed her job.

Once she had left, Ormonde adopted a more co-operative tone, although he still didn't invite either of them to take a seat.

'Now that she's gone, I can be more frank with you, officer. I *was* in Swindon that evening, but visiting a lady friend of mine. I travelled up there on an earlier evening train in order to keep the assignation and was somewhat delayed in getting back. There were no local trains available back to Kemble by then, so I hired a coach.'

'And the name of the lady in question?' Jack enquired as he spoke for the first time, notebook open and pencil poised.

'I'm afraid I don't remember,' was all Ormonde could manage by way of reply.

'Let me assist you,' Percy replied coldly. 'Her name was Martha Longhurst and I've already spoken to her. You paid her, but not for her "personal" services, shall we say? You bribed her to say that you'd been with her for two hours.'

'That was to cover up who I'd *really* been with,' Ormonde explained hastily. 'She's a lady whose husband is a man of some importance in Swindon and were our association to be known...'

'A lady so well known that you can't remember her name?' Percy fired back.

'And despite the fact,' Jack threw in for good measure, 'that your coachman saw you leaving after supper that evening, shortly after Miss Ormonde, and at a time that the only remaining train would have been the same one as hers?'

'Let's dispense with the lies shall we, Mr Ormonde?' Percy demanded in an icy tone, with a facial expression resembling a stone-mason's chisel. 'You were on the train with your sister, in the same carriage, and the same compartment, when she fell to her death. Your only reason for denying that must be that you were the cause of that fall. Do you have any response to that allegation?'

'Get out of my salon!' Ormonde demanded as he seemed to regain his composure and bluster. 'Get out and stay out! Don't come back unless it's to arrest me, and when and if you do I'll have the finest solicitor in London here with me. Now go!'

As they stood back out on the pavement, Jack turned to Percy. 'Still no confession. The man's obviously determined to bluff it out.'

'Let's see if he can survive Esther's little surprise,' Percy chuckled as they walked back up the street.

Esther couldn't help but hear the final heated exchange downstairs and she took this God-given opportunity to slip the crumpled scarf from her shopping bag. She hurried over to the dressing table, selected a large bottle from the 'Tuberose' collection and tipped a generous quantity over the scarf before retreating behind her desk and leaning down over her accounts book as she tried to block out the almost overpowering smell of the perfume.

Less than a minute later she heard Ormonde mounting the stairs and he appeared in the doorway.

'In case you were wondering...' he began, then his face set in wide-eyed horror as he breathed in the all too familiar smell. He looked across towards the dressing table, gave a strangled cry and raced over to it. He grabbed the crumpled scarf that had once been Marianne's gag, then turned furiously to confront Esther. 'You did this, didn't you?'

'Did what, sir?'

'Put this on the dressing table. It wasn't here earlier, so you must have put it there. And where's that perfume stink coming from?'

'What perfume?' Esther replied in the most rational tone she could manage, just as Ormonde leapt at her with a shriek.

'It's all been happening since you arrived here! You won't shake me, understand? I'll kill you first!' He had his hands around her throat and Esther was having increasing difficulty breathing. Just as the room began to swim before her eyes, she was aware of Abigail standing in the bedroom doorway.

'Mr Ormonde — what are you doing?' she demanded. Esther slipped into unconsciousness.

Chapter Fourteen

Esther came round on the bed in the room she had been working in for the past few weeks, to find a strange middle-aged man examining her chest through her unfastened bodice and blouse, the straps of her chemise pulled to one side. She began to struggle until the man murmured reassuring words, and from behind him appeared the concerned face of Abigail Prendergast.

'It's alright, Esther — he's a doctor. I called him in for you, and Mr Ormonde can pay.'

The doctor lifted his head from where he had been examining Esther's chest.

'There doesn't appear to be anything to cause concern,' he assured them both. 'A day or so's rest should see you back to normal health. Your pulse is strong and your breathing's regular. What happened, exactly? And how did you get those red marks around your neck?'

'I'm not sure,' Esther lied as the memory of being attacked by Ormonde came flooding back and she looked wildly around the room, which appeared to be empty apart from Abigail and the doctor, who was closing his medical bag and appeared to be preparing to leave.

'At least twenty-four hours' bed rest,' he instructed them. Then he looked back down at Esther. 'None of my business, of course, but perhaps you'd be best to report this to the police. Those marks did not come naturally.'

'There's a police officer downstairs already,' Abigail assured him as she led him down the stairs and out through the front door. 'If you send your account to Mr Ormonde here at the gallery, I'll ensure that it's paid. Just give her a moment to get dressed,' she instructed the police officer as she walked through the salon and back up the stairs, where Esther lay staring at the ceiling. She was trying to gather her thoughts, wondering how best to react to the attack on her by Ormonde and how it might affect her undercover operation.

'What on earth provoked that?' Abigail asked Esther as she sat on the edge of the bed, watching her refastening her clothing. 'Did he catch you trying to steal some of that perfume? The room reeks of it.'

'No,' Esther replied with a feigned expression of incomprehension. 'He was over at the dressing table, then he turned round, accused me of placing something on there, then attacked me for no obvious reason. His eyes were really weird, like some sort of maniac, and if you hadn't come along when you did, I'd probably be dead now.'

'I'd just got back in after visiting the printers and those police officers were on their way down the street — or at least, one of them was. The younger one seemed to be hanging around across the road. Anyway, I heard the terrible shouting and what sounded like Mr Ormonde threatening to kill you, and I rushed upstairs. When he saw me, he let you go, pushed past me and ran all the way out of the salon. He hasn't been back since, but I dragged you onto the bed, then went back outside and got that young Scotland Yard man to call the doctor and then come back here. He's waiting downstairs to take your statement, but I imagine that we'll both be out of a job after this.'

'I'm not sure I could tackle those stairs at the moment,' Esther lied as she made a big display of running her hand over her brow. 'Could you ask the police officer to come up here, please?' She saw the hesitation on Abigail's face and hastened to reassure her. 'As long as you're down in the tea room at the foot of the stairs, I'm sure my reputation won't be compromised, even though he *is* good looking, as you say.'

Abigail descended the stairs and Esther heard her instructing someone that 'the young lady upstairs' was very weak and would need to be transported home, so it would be necessary for the officer to keep his questions brief. Then Esther lay back on the bed and tried to keep the smile off her face, just in case, as Jack came clomping up the staircase, looked behind him, rushed to her side and grabbed her hand.

'Are you alright?' he asked, loving concern written all over his face.

'Perfectly,' Esther assured him in a whisper, 'if a little sore around the neck. Ormonde tried to strangle me when I put the gag on the dressing table. I notice that it's gone now, so he must have taken it with him.'

'Is the baby alright?' Jack asked nervously.

'As far as I can tell,' Esther assured him, 'but I need to get home. There's no way I can stay here after this, whatever you and Uncle Percy may say. Ormonde seems to have run away.'

'Never mind about him,' Jack insisted. 'It's *you* I care about. I just want to get you home and Uncle Percy can piss in his hat if he thinks you're going to be involved in this for one day longer.'

Esther chuckled at Jack's crude language, only to be reminded that her neck hurt. 'You'd better get your notebook out and pretend that I'm making a formal complaint, in case Abigail decides to play the chaperone,' she advised Jack, who duly obliged.

'Actually,' he said, 'it might suit us very nicely if you do make a formal complaint. It'll give us an excuse for arresting him, then we can light a blowtorch under him regarding what he did to his sister.'

'How come you were still outside?' Esther asked as she stroked his arm. 'I'm glad you were, in case there's any doubt on that score.'

'I just had a bad feeling,' Jack replied. 'Uncle Percy's methods are a bit excessive and it seemed likely that Ormonde would over-react when you pulled the trick with the gag. Good job I hung back and that Miss Abigail remembered me by sight.'

'I think your face is already embroidered on her heart,' Esther grimaced back up at him, 'and that sounds like her coming back up. Better start looking like a guardian of the law again, instead of my husband.'

Abigail reappeared in the doorway and Jack made a great pretence of assuring Esther that a cable would be sent to every police station in London, seeking the apprehension of a man suspected of the attempted murder of one of his employees.

'Rest assured, Miss, we won't leave a stone unturned,' he told her, as he looked round and appeared to become aware of Abigail's return.

'Could you summon a cab, please? I'll escort this young lady to her home and ensure that nothing else happens to her, then I'll come back and take your statement.'

'I'll make sure I have tea and biscuits waiting for you,' Abigail said, smiling invitingly as she took Esther's other arm, and between them they escorted her gingerly down the stairs. She was placed in the chair in front of the salon counter and while they waited for Abigail to summon a cab Jack gazed up at the "Ophelia" painting, still in pride of place on the wall.

'She *does* look a bit like Lucy, doesn't she?' Esther observed as she followed Jack's gaze.

Jack frowned. 'Unfortunately for Lucy, yes she does. I think my mad uncle has some scheme in mind for getting her involved as well. But for you, this is the final day of your employment here, believe me.'

Alice Bridges made the predictable fussing noises as Jack opened the front door to their rooms and led Esther gingerly down the hallway with one hand supporting her arm.

'God love us, what happened to you?' Alice said as she took in the livid red weals on Esther's neck.

'It's a long story,' Jack replied, 'but it would seem that Esther will be home for a while, so we can relieve you of baby-minding duties until further notice. Thank you *so* much for all you've done. Are you sure we don't owe you anything?'

Alice shook her head. 'Definitely not. It was a pure pleasure to look after the dear little thing and if you ever need anyone to look after her in the future, do please think of me first.'

'We will, Alice, and thank you again,' Esther assured her. 'Why don't you come down here for tea tomorrow morning, and let me do my best to explain it all to you?'

As the front door closed behind her, Esther reached up and kissed Jack. 'Thank you, my knight in shining armour. Now lead me to our daughter, who nearly became motherless.'

As they stood there holding hands like two young sweethearts, gazing adoringly down at their peacefully sleeping daughter, Esther began to tremble, then burst into tears. Jack lowered her into a chair and knelt down to hold her reassuringly in his arms.

'It's delayed shock,' he advised her. 'We see it a lot in accident victims.'

'It's true, isn't it?' Esther sobbed. 'If Abigail hadn't been there, I'd be dead and poor sweet little Lily wouldn't have a mother. *Please* don't make me go back to that dreadful place and that sick lunatic!'

'That's one thing you can rest assured of,' Jack replied consolingly. 'If Uncle Percy tries to insist, I'll simply resign from the force and become a coalman, like you suggested.'

Esther gazed up at him through a haze of drying tears. 'You'd really do that for me?'

'Of *course* I would. You're the most important person in my life. You and Lily, of course. The Yard is just how I earn my living, and there's more than one way of doing that.'

'But while you're still a police officer,' Esther reminded him, 'you have to go back to Ormonde's salon and have tea and biscuits with that rather entrancing Abigail, who's clearly set her sights on you.'

'I suppose I do,' Jack conceded, 'but I'd rather stay here with you. However, the "entrancing Abigail", as you call her, will get suspicious if I'm delayed too long.'

Shortly after five pm, Jack answered the knock on the door and a massive bunch of flowers was thrust into his face. He burst out laughing and looked out into the hallway at the crestfallen face of his uncle, who also appeared to be armed with a large wine bottle.

'You'll need more than that if you expect Esther to allow you in,' Jack advised Percy.

'At least three helpings of that delicious fish and fried potatoes that you employed to seduce me into getting involved in your madcap schemes,' Esther insisted from behind Jack. 'I'll put the oven on, and don't even *think* of showing your face back here without them.'

An hour and a half later the silence was palpable enough to be photographed and Esther felt guiltily aware that she was the cause of it. She reached across the table and rested a hand on Percy's wrist. 'I'll forgive you, provided that we're agreed that I'm finished at the art salon.'

'I think everyone is,' Percy assured her, 'including that sweet young thing who worked there legitimately.'

'That "sweet young thing" had designs on Jack,' Esther pouted, 'but has the salon closed down already?'

'It can't continue without Ormonde himself, I imagine,' Percy pointed out, 'and there's been no indication that he's about to resume business. We have men posted to look out for his return, but so far without any success.'

'You were too late,' Jack advised him. 'When I went back to take the statement from Abigail Prendergast, she told me that Ormonde showed up around the middle of the day, ran upstairs, came back down with a couple of heavy looking travelling bags, told Miss Prendergast to lock the salon and take a month's wages out of the petty cash drawer, then headed off in a cab in the direction of Holborn.'

'I'll take a guess that he was heading for his country retreat in Wiltshire,' Percy said, nodding, 'which is precisely where we want him.'

'So I'm finished at the salon?' Esther asked anxiously.

Percy nodded. 'Indeed you are, my dear, with the grateful thanks of Scotland Yard for all your invaluable assistance.'

'I'm not sure I achieved anything, apart from exposing that abortionist,' Esther replied with a frown.

'He was arrested and charged two days ago,' Percy advised her. 'I don't think we'll need you to give evidence against him, but if you do we'll make sure that the court's left in no doubt that you weren't really seeking an abortion.'

'You'll actually admit that Scotland Yard was obliged to rely on a mere woman?' Esther said sarcastically and Percy smiled.

'The day is not long away when we'll actually employ them, but not necessarily for the sort of work you did for us. There's an increase in the number of complaints from women prisoners alleging that they were groped inappropriately by male officers while being taken into custody.'

'I hope neither of you indulge in anything like that,' Esther replied frostily and Percy grinned back at her.

'Believe me, what we have to endure from the women we arrest is far worse than what we're alleged to do to them. I've lost count of the number of times I've been kneed in the unmentionables.'

Esther looked at Jack with raised eyebrows and he nodded.

'A couple of times,' he admitted. 'Plus I've been offered all sorts of sexual services in exchange for releasing them. None of which I accepted, let me hasten to add.'

'You'd better not, if *you* want to avoid an injury,' Esther threatened him with a mock scowl.

'Anyway, Uncle,' Jack enquired, if only to change the topic of conversation, 'do you still need me on the Ormonde case, and if not, what am I likely to find waiting for me when I report back for duty tomorrow?'

'You're going nowhere near Whitehall yet, my boy,' Percy assured him. 'We haven't finished with Ormonde by a long chalk.'

'Presumably we'll be journeying down to Wiltshire in order to arrest him for the attack on Esther?'

'Yes, but not yet,' Percy replied with a slow grin. 'We'll let him stew out there for a while, but by the time we take him into custody I'll have another nasty surprise lined up for him.'

'Not involving my wife, I hope?' Jack enquired.

'No — your sister,' Percy replied with a conspiratorial wink.

Jack's draw dropped. 'Mother will hang your guts on her washing line if you expose Lucy to the sort of danger that Esther experienced. And she'd no doubt do so already if I peached on you regarding Esther's brush with a lunatic.'

'What I have in mind for Lucy will not bring her face to face with Ormonde, you may rest assured of that,' Percy replied with a self-satisfied smirk. 'At least, not in the flesh.'

'What exactly are you planning?' Esther demanded. 'Quite apart from being my sister-in-law, she's a very good friend, and Jack's mother won't be the only one after your guts if you harm a hair on her head.'

'You can both breathe more easily,' Percy smiled reassuringly. 'But you would admit, would you not, that being confronted with objects associated with his heinous deed makes Ormonde very nervous?'

'I think the marks that are still visible on my neck attest to that,' Esther replied acidly.

'Precisely,' Percy continued. 'So how do you think he'd react to being confronted with Marianne herself?'

'You're going to dig up her corpse and dump it on his doorstep?' Esther asked sarcastically, while Jack sat there expressionless.

'Not quite,' Percy replied, still smiling like someone who'd won a fortune at the races. 'Are we not also agreed that Ormonde's become convinced that he's haunted by the restless spirit of his victim?'

'Yes, so what?' Esther said.

'Well, how do you think he'd react to being confronted by her ghost?'

It went deathly quiet, as Esther rose from the table and began collecting the plates.

'You're madder than even I imagined,' she replied bluntly.

Jack winced and smiled apologetically across at Percy, who seemed not to be in the slightest bit offended as he replied confidently, 'As someone recently said to me — "Oh ye of little faith". Jack, from memory, describe the layout of the Booking Hall of Kemble Station.'

Jack closed his eyes and described his recollection of it. 'There's a fairly large open section as you go in, with a bench down the right hand wall. Then, to the left, there's a wall with a window that looks into the area where the ticket-seller-cum-porter sits, selling tickets. And that's about all I can remember.'

'That's all you *need* to remember,' Percy advised him. 'But you'd agree with me that the window between the two allows passengers to look into the ticket seller's room, while at the same time allowing the ticket seller to look out into the Booking Hall, and that you have to pass through that booking hall to get to the platforms?'

'Yes, but so what?'

'I'll collect you at ten in the morning, young Jack,' Percy advised him as he rose to leave. 'Then we're off to see a woman about a ghost.'

Chapter Fifteen

'Cable from Scotland Yard, Sergeant,' Constable Jacks advised Joe Oakley as he walked in from his home two doors up the street. Oakley took the paper from him and studied it with an irritated frown.

'They don't ask much, do they? Confirm that he's back in residence, keep 'im under discreet observation, alert the Yard immediately if 'e shows any sign o' movin' out, and above all don't alert 'is suspicions. I suppose it'll make a change from breakin' up pub brawls and catchin' poachers, but 'ow much manpower do they think we've got at our disposal down 'ere?'

'D'yer want me ter see to that, Sergeant?'

'No thanks, lad. The cable said "discreet". Yer about as discreet as Bill Tansley's prize bull when it's 'on 'eat. Leave the clever stuff ter yer superiors.'

'Yes, Sergeant.'

'I don't s'pose yer've seen 'im around 'ere lately?'

'No, Sergeant.'

'Well, I'll try the station first. Then maybe a quiet word wi' Bert Gregson.'

'Yes, Sergeant.'

'Right, get the pot on fer tea, then I'm off ter the station.'

Within the hour Sergeant Oakley had learned that the man that Scotland Yard wished to have placed under discreet surveillance had passed through Kemble Station two days earlier, dragging two heavy travelling bags, had tipped the porter generously for his assistance in loading them onto a wagon waiting hopefully in the forecourt for passing trade, and had instructed the driver to take him to Sandpool Farm, where he remained, so far as anyone was aware. Later that evening Oakley wandered in plain clothes up to the farm itself, lost ten shillings to Bert Gregson in card games that he put down to expenses, and cabled back to London that their man was where they had suspected him of being.

'Avaunt and quit my sight!' Hilda Fancourt bellowed from the stage as the two men walked down through the stalls. 'We're in the middle of a lighting rehearsal and Iago is about to get his come-uppance. It had better be good!'

'It is,' Percy assured her as he reminded her that the young man with him was the brother of her leading lady, who confirmed that assertion by jumping four feet down off the stage and embracing them both enthusiastically.

'Uncle Percy — *and* Jack — don't tell me you've acquired an interest in the theatre? Or are you perhaps here to watch me rehearse without having to buy a ticket for the public performances themselves? And why are you free to attend during the working day? Shouldn't you be out catching criminals?'

'That's several questions at once,' Percy replied with a grin, while Jack left the explanations to him. 'And the answer to them all is "yes". Yes, we are here out of interest in the theatre, yes we do want to see you perform, yes we are at work, and yes we are seeking to buckle a serious criminal.'

When Lucy remained silent, the smile slowly fading as she tried to absorb it all, Percy extracted the photograph of Edgar and Marianne Ormonde and handed it to her.

'We require your assistance to capture *him*, for which we require that you look as much as possible like *her*.'

Lucy looked with an experienced eye at the image of Marianne, then smiled. 'Give me ten minutes,' she offered.

Percy raised his hand to detain her. 'Not now. And not here.'

'When and where?'

'That will depend upon what your stage manager can arrange,' Percy explained. 'I don't see her on stage at present.'

'She's probably up in the lighting gallery, checking the look of her sets under the unforgiving bright lights,' Lucy suggested.

'She was, but now she's down here among the paying audience,' came a voice familiar to Percy, and he turned round to smile ingratiatingly at Frances Fordyce.

'Allow me to introduce my nephew and Lucy's brother, Jack, who's also, by a happy coincidence, an officer employed by Scotland Yard. Jack, this lady, with assistance from Lucy, is going to produce the ghost of Marianne Ormonde.'

'You've decided to go ahead then?' Frances asked, smiling, and Percy nodded.

'We have, but it will require a good deal of organisation and not a little inconvenience. We all have to travel to a small township north of Swindon and we have to set up our operation during the hours of darkness. As I understand it, we'll require two substantial mirrors, a co-operative railway employee, the acting talents of my niece, and a certain amount of theatrical make-up.'

'When?' was Frances's only question, while Lucy began to make domestic excuses, which Percy waved aside.

'Your children will be none the worse for being looked after by a successful architect for a day or so and when you return triumphant, they'll be all the more overjoyed at your renewed presence, and may even behave themselves.'

'We open in two weeks,' Lucy reminded him.

'This will be over in two days,' Percy assured her. 'Allow for at least two nights at a hotel in Swindon, a *very* busy day setting up what I believe you actors call the "set", and a very dramatic evening that will end in the arrest of a self-confessed murderer.'

'If he's confessed, why do we need to set what I suspect is a trap?' Frances asked.

'What makes you think that?' Percy said innocently, to which Frances replied with a conspiratorial smile, 'I know my Shakespeare. It's Hamlet who delivers the line "The play's the thing wherein I'll catch the conscience of a king". You're hoping that a ghost will wring a confession out of a suspect, aren't you?'

'Once again, your astuteness humbles me,' Percy replied with genuine gallantry, and Frances smiled as her glance dropped to the floor.

'At least it'll save you the effort of beating it out of him with your billy clubs,' she parried.

'Most of this is escaping me,' Lucy complained. 'I believe I'm being cast as the ghost of a murder victim in order to confront her killer in the belief that he'll confess. Aren't you rather placing me in danger? I have two children, remember.'

'You won't be face to face with him,' Jack explained. 'At least, that's what Uncle Percy assures me.'

'Indeed she won't,' Frances confirmed. 'As I understand it, Lucy will appear courtesy of Pepper's Ghost?'

'Exactly.' Percy smiled at Lucy reassuringly.

'And this all takes place in Swindon, you say?' Lucy asked. 'And will take two days? What costume will I require?'

'That will be supplied,' Percy explained.

'At a guess, from the original corpse?' Frances said, at which Lucy let out a ladylike scream.

Percy turned to wag an admonitory finger at Frances. 'There are times when astuteness can prove unwise, madam, and I believe that was one of them.'

'I can't believe that Lucy was insane enough to agree,' Esther complained as Jack broke the news and explained the plan insofar as he was fully aware of it.

'You know how persuasive Uncle Percy can be,' Jack reminded her, 'and Lucy just can't resist a bit of melodrama.'

'Did he tell her that the man tried to strangle the life out of me just for putting a scarf on a bedside table?' she demanded.

Jack shook his head. 'What do *you* think? He played the "public duty" card, and filled her head with all the melodrama that she'd be a part of. "Bringing a cold-blooded murderer to his just deserts" was his precise phrase. She was even disappointed that she wouldn't have any lines to deliver and would just have to stand there looking malevolent.'

'Rather her than me, all the same.' Esther shuddered. 'So when does all this take place?'

'This coming Sunday, most likely. We're travelling down there on the Saturday and we'll do what's called a "dress rehearsal" that evening, then the real thing on the Sunday evening, when there's only the one train back to London.'

'And do you *really* have to go?'

'I'm afraid I do. I'll be the one leading Ormonde over the trapdoor, so to speak.'

'Jack, *please* promise me you'll take care!' Esther pleaded with him as she hugged him to her. 'The man's a raving maniac.'

'All I have to do is arrest him on the charge of assaulting you. I'll have a local police sergeant with me and he's built like the King's Cross gasometer. I just walk Ormonde into the station Booking Hall and Percy and Lucy take over from there. Once we have his screaming confession the sergeant will buckle him and Percy and I will bring him back in the local police coach, with a couple of local bobbies for additional muscle.'

'And what if he *doesn't* confess?'

'We'll arrest him anyway, for the attempted murder on you. Either way we'll be bringing him back and a few months in Newgate should soften him up.'

Esher took his face in her hands and kissed him gently on the lips. 'One of the reasons I love you, Jack Enright, is because you're not like all the other police officers. Not like your Uncle Percy, determined to get their man at all costs. Not like those cosh-wielding thugs who break heads in pub fights. You care about ordinary people and you became a policeman to protect them. Don't get just like all the rest of Scotland Yard, promise me?'

'I promise,' Jack replied, suitably chastised.

Chapter Sixteen

The large and ponderous police coach rumbled up to the Horse and Hounds and stopped. The coachman climbed from his footboard and stepped down onto the uneven roadway before opening the door for the four passengers he had conveyed all the way from London to Swindon along indifferent roads and through changeable weather. First out was Percy Enright and he held out his hand for Frances Fordyce, who bowed her head in gracious acknowledgment as she stepped down, leaving Jack to perform the same service for his sister Lucy.

'What about the cargo, Sergeant?' the coachman enquired as they all stood uncertainly on the pavement outside the best hotel in that market town. Percy nodded towards the two cheval mirrors inside the coach, both of them carefully covered in heavy blankets and propped up against the seats.

'I need to escort the ladies inside and claim our accommodation. Unload our bags from the roof first, then while we're inside keep a watchful eye on those two mirrors. I'll be back out shortly to direct you where to go next.'

'Very good, Sergeant. Will you be long? Only I thought I might chance lighting up my pipe.'

'Good idea. I'll probably join you when I come back out. It'll be just me and the Constable for the next stage, anyway.'

The lady behind the reception desk confirmed that two double rooms had indeed been reserved by telegraph from Scotland Yard the previous day and the boy stepped forward to take their bags.

'Take the ladies' baggage up first,' Percy instructed the boy, who nodded eagerly and picked up the two overnight bags with their labels. Percy smiled at Frances and Lucy. 'I suggest that you two ladies freshen up, then spend the afternoon resting. We had an early start and we have a busy evening ahead of us before we can relax with a late supper. Johnson will be back to pick you up at around six this evening.'

Back outside, Percy joined the coachman for a smoke, after checking that the mirrors were where he had left them propped up inside the coach and appeared to be undamaged.

'Why couldn't we simply have acquired mirrors here in Swindon?' Jack asked.

Percy smiled condescendingly. 'We couldn't guarantee that this sheep market of a town was supplied with a furniture store of sufficient quality. Those mirrors are on hire from Regent Street, which is why I don't want them damaged in any way, hence the covers on them and the discomfort they caused during our journey down here, when they were resting against our legs. And I for one didn't fancy lugging them on and off a train, before you ask why we had to endure the discomfort of a coach journey.'

'This operation must be costing a small fortune,' Jack commented. 'I hope you got the Chief Inspector's approval.'

'Almost,' Percy replied with a conspiratorial smile, 'I told him that we were moving in to arrest Ormonde on suspicion, but I don't think he fully appreciated what we're going to be doing exactly, or how much it's going to cost.'

'Let's hope we finish up getting our man.'

'Amen to that. Now, Johnson, if you've finished your fill, head to the railway station. It's directly down the main street here, then off to the right.'

'Why Swindon Station and not Kemble?' Jack enquired.

'Because we need to renew our acquaintance with the obliging Mr Babbage.'

'The local coachman? Why do we need him, when we've got a coach of our own?' Jack asked, genuinely puzzled.

'Because the coach we brought from London screams "Metropolitan Police", that's why. I want our return to Kemble to be less obvious, since we don't know who'll be watching our movements, do we?'

'Did you alert the local sergeant?'

'I most certainly did and he'll be awaiting our arrival. But before we get to that stage, let's concentrate on the immediate one. Ah, here we are.'

The two men stepped down from their coach in the area reserved for public carriages and had little difficulty in locating Josh Babbage as he sat on the front board of his own coach, reigns in hand and pipe in mouth. He smiled as he saw them approach and recognised them.

'Afternoon, gents. Another trip ter Kemble?'

'Several, probably,' Percy advised him. 'We'll need you on a permanent basis until late tomorrow evening — shall we say thirty pounds for the entire period?'

'Fer thirty quid I'll drive yer through the gates o' Hell.'

'Kemble will probably be sufficient,' Percy replied drily. 'You might wish to begin by assisting our existing coachman to lift those two mirrors out of his coach into yours, very carefully. Then we're taking them to Kemble. We don't want to arrive there before dark, so if you want to take us on a vacationer's tour of the local countryside first, that will be fine.'

Having introduced one coachman to the other, he instructed Scotland Yard coachman Johnson to return to Swindon Station at six-thirty that evening with Mrs Fordyce and Mrs Wilton, and hand them over to Josh Babbage, who'd be driving them to Kemble Station. Then he bid good afternoon to Johnson and instructed Babbage to begin the journey to Kemble.

It was just beginning to get dark as Jack and Percy alighted outside Kemble Police Station and instructed Babbage to wait for them to re-emerge. Inside, Sergeant Oakley was impatiently awaiting them, one eye on the clock on the wall as he envisaged his supper slowly congealing on the stove two doors up. He came through eagerly when they arrived at the front desk and ushered them hastily into the back room.

'Everything's laid out just as yer instructed, Sergeant.'

'Excellent,' Percy murmured as he walked over to the long table where the property found on the body of Marianne Ormonde had been laid out, and held up a blood-soaked dress.

'Do you think that will fit Lucy without the need to call in a tailor?' he asked Jack, who wrinkled his nose in disgust.

'The more appropriate question is whether or not Lucy will deign to wear it. It stinks!'

'Good point,' Percy observed as he fished around in the deceased's purse and came up with a scent spray. Holding it out at arm's length to assist his ageing eyes he smiled. 'This should overcome her squeamishness. "Tuberose", wasn't it?'

He sprayed a little on the dress and Jack sneezed loudly.

'Esther wasn't exaggerating about that stuff — it's overpowering!'

'Better than the smell of two week old blood,' Percy observed as he studied the dress more carefully. 'A lot of the blood will be fully visible even on a head and shoulders view. It must have come from her head, which from memory was quite a mess.'

'Yes, don't remind me,' Jack muttered as he turned away and caught Sergeant Oakley studying his fob watch. 'Do we need the sergeant any longer?'

Percy looked back up from studying the blood-spattered dress. 'Yes, sorry for keeping you from an early supper, Sergeant. Before you go, any news of Mr Ormonde's movements?'

'Accordin' ter Gregson 'e went shootin' on Thursday and made a short visit ter Martha Longhurst 'ere in the village on Friday mornin'. Otherwise nothin' to speak o', but Bert promised ter let me know immediately if there's any sign of 'im makin' a run fer it.'

'Fine,' Percy confirmed. 'Do you happen to know what time Michael Parsons clocks on for duty at the station?'

'Around six in the evenin', usually. 'E does twelve hour nights an' 'e finishes at six in the mornin'.'

'So he should be on duty around now?'

'I'd imagine so.'

'Very well, let's find out for ourselves, shall we? Thanks for your invaluable assistance, Sergeant, and tomorrow evening at approximately this time you'll be assisting Scotland Yard in the apprehension of a murderer.'

'Might lead ter me gettin' more respect from some o' the locals who seem ter think that me only function in life's ter spoil their fun an' games,' Oakley said, grinning as he took his leave.

Percy and Jack instructed Babbage to drive them down the main street to Kemble Station, where they unloaded the mirrors in the small forecourt, then instructed Babbage to return to Swindon and come back with the two ladies who Johnson would be delivering to him in the police coach. Then they wheeled the mirrors into the Booking Hall by means of the cradles on which they were mounted and knocked loudly on the door to the ticket seller's office, which was opened by a rather grumpy Michael Parsons.

'What do you want *this* time?' he demanded gruffly.

'Information and co-operation,' Percy advised him with a stern stare, 'and remember that I'm still in a position to end your promising career.'

'So you keep reminding me,' Parsons grumbled. 'So what is it you need?'

'First of all, confirm that the Scotland Yard copy of your timetable is still up to date, and that there's only one train out of here for London late tomorrow evening — Sunday.'

'That's right,' Parsons confirmed. 'The nine fifteen — all stations from Chelmsford.'

'And how well patronised is it?' Percy asked next.

'Depends,' Parsons replied uncertainly. 'Some Sundays there's nobody at all, some Sundays we may get two or three. On public holidays it's more like ten or so.'

'And the only way onto the platform is through this Booking Hall?'

'There's a gate at the end of the "up" platform back there,' Parsons indicated with a nod of the head, 'but if people need to buy a ticket then yes, they'd have to come through here.'

'But if the gas lamps were extinguished and the doors were closed, they'd back-track to that gate you just mentioned and buy their ticket when they got off at Paddington?'

'Yes, but that would be somewhat unauthorised.'

'So's murder,' Percy replied laconically as he glanced up at the ticket window. 'Jack, take one of these mirrors into the Booking Hall out there, place it somewhere near the corner, but facing the entrance at a forty-five degree angle, then take the cover off it and turn off the gas lamps in there.'

'What if we get customers needing to buy a ticket?' Parsons objected.

'Just tell them that the rail company's experimenting with new decor,' Percy suggested, 'but we won't be long. While we're waiting, can you look out some chalk for me?'

Jack manoeuvred the first mirror roughly into position and removed the heavy blanket, then walked round the room and extinguished the gas jets, leaving only the light flooding in through the hatch from the ticket seller's office and the more diffused glow from the platform lights.

'Now what?' he yelled through the window to Percy, who'd uncovered the mirror inside the office and was pointing it at an angle out through the window.

'Let me know when you can see my hand,' Percy shouted back to Jack.

Several manoeuvres and a few curses later, Jack confirmed that he could see Percy's hand and Percy stepped fully in front of the mirror.

'Now what can you see?'

'You, but only vaguely,' Jack replied. 'There's too much light coming through from the platform.'

'Go and extinguish the nearest gas jets on either side of the platform entrance,' Percy instructed him.

Jack did as he was told and then came back into the Booking Hall and took another look. 'That's good,' he announced, 'but it's still a bit hazy.'

'All the better.' Percy grinned to himself, just as Frances and Lucy entered the Booking Hall and Frances observed 'Bloody amateurs' before walking through the communicating door and smiling at Percy.

'Thank goodness you invited me along,' she observed. 'The lighting's all wrong. You need the bright light shining on the *subject*, not the mirror. May I?'

159

'Be my guest,' Percy invited her as he stood to one side.

'Lucy,' Frances instructed her, 'go and stand in front of that mirror. Stay where you are, Jack,' she added as she yelled through the communication hatch, then turned to look at Michael Parsons. 'I take it from your uniform that you work here. Do your employers by any chance issue you with a lantern?'

'There's one back here, somewhere,' Parsons responded, without it even occurring to him that this bossy lady was in no way authorised to either give him instructions or commandeer company property.

'Good,' Frances responded. 'Light it up and place it on a stand to the side of this young lady.'

Parsons did as instructed and Lucy's image suddenly became clearer in the facing mirror.

'That's a whole lot better!' Jack yelled through the window and Frances reached forward and adjusted the hinge where the glass met the supporting frame, tilting the reflection upwards.

'Let me know when you've got just the head and shoulders!' she commanded and Jack duly obliged when that point was reached. 'That seems to be the best we can do, given these rather makeshift conditions,' she advised Percy. 'Now, can we get back for that late supper you promised us?'

'Not quite yet,' Percy advised her. 'We need to put all the lights back on and mark the positions of the mirrors with chalk marks. We can't leave them where they are for twenty-four hours, and tomorrow evening, when we do the real thing, we won't have the luxury of time.'

Once the chalk marks were made, Percy turned to Michael Parsons. 'Leave a note for your daytime colleague that those chalk marks are not to be removed in an excess of cleaning zeal. The mirrors can be explained as lost property. I'll certainly be glad to lose them when all this is over. We're leaving now, but we'll be back at the same time tomorrow. You had better be here.'

Chapter Seventeen

At shortly before seven the following evening, Jack and Sergeant Oakley left Constable Jacks with the police coach at the entrance to Sandpool Farm and walked down the driveway as silently as the circumstances permitted. As they approached the rear of the main house, Bert Gregson sidled out from the coach house.

''E's still in there, Joe,' he advised Sergeant Oakley while nodding politely to Jack. 'Florrie Bradfield went 'ome a few minutes since — yer musta passed 'er on yer way in — so Clarice's prob'ly servin' the supper.'

Oakley hammered hard on the back door, and after a few moments a light shone in the scullery, the door opened, and there stood Clarice Battersby in a long black dress with a white serving apron.

'We need ter see yer master, Clarice,' Oakley advised her gently.

'I'm afraid 'e's at 'is supper,' she replied.

'We don't care if he's at his prayers,' Jack replied sternly. 'Let us in.'

Clarice stood meekly to one side and Oakley and Jack strode purposefully through the scullery and kitchen, down the hallway and through the open door to the dining room, where Ormonde looked up with a mixture of surprise and annoyance.

'I told the girl I wasn't to be disturbed,' he insisted.

'Well, this should you disturb you alright,' Jack replied angrily as he remembered what Esther had suffered at the hands of this pompous balloon. 'Edgar Ormonde, I'm arresting you for the attempted murder of Esther Enright.'

'And who might she be?' Ormonde demanded haughtily.

'You probably knew her as Esther Jacobs,' Jack replied with all the patience he could muster, 'but her real name's "Enright", and she's been closely watching your behaviour for the past few weeks, before you attempted to strangle her to death. She won't be returning to work, by the way.'

'This is ridiculous!' Ormonde objected. 'Whatever that idiot girl's alleging is a lie.'

'That "idiot girl", as you call her, is my wife,' Jack replied angrily, 'and please do me the courtesy of resisting arrest, so that I can belt blue blazes out of your greasy self-satisfied mug.'

'Steady on, sir,' Oakley warned him.

'"Sir?"' Ormonde echoed in disbelief, 'you're addressing this self-inflated pipsqueak as "sir"?'

'He's Scotland Yard, sir, an' I 'as ter do what I'm told by them folk up in London. An' right now, I'm instructed ter take yer in charge on a count o' attempted murder.'

'I demand to speak to a senior officer!' Ormonde insisted.

'All in good time,' Jack advised him through gritted teeth, 'although you'll no doubt be concerned to learn that he's also related to the woman you tried to strangle.'

'May I finish my supper first?'

'No, you may not,' Jack advised him with a sadistic grin. 'A shame really, because although I've never had occasion to taste it, they tell me that Newgate fare doesn't run to chicken.'

'May I at least get my coat and hat?' Ormonde requested, slightly less sure of his ground.

'Certainly,' Jack replied with mock politeness, 'although of course your deerstalker bonnet's no longer available to you, is it?'

Somewhat pale in the face, Ormonde rose from the supper table, dabbed his upper lip with a napkin to soak up the beads of perspiration that had just formed above his top lip and headed towards the door that led to the corridor.

'I'll just come wi' yer, sir,' Oakley advised him with appropriate deference, 'just so's yer don't try jumpin' out o' the winder.'

As the three of them re-emerged from the back door into the laneway that led back to the police coach, Oakley spoke quietly in Ormonde's ear. 'By rights I should be tyin' yer 'ands be'ind yer back, sir, but if yer promises ter come quiet like, there'll be no need o' that.'

'But if you do make a run for it, I'd welcome the opportunity to grind your face into the dirt of your own driveway,' Jack muttered ominously.

Back at Kemble Station, matters were progressing smoothly. Lucy had reappeared from the Ladies' Waiting Room along the platform, dressed in the costume retrieved from Marianne Ormonde's corpse and protesting vociferously at the foul smell that was coming off it. Percy and Frances had placed the mirrors on the chalk marks and Michael Parsons had obligingly extinguished the gas lamps in the Booking Hall and most of the "up" platform. The only light was now coming from inside his office, where the mirror had been covered back over with one of the blankets and Frances had supervised the total blacking of Lucy's eyes, including the lids when she closed them as instructed. Finally, the thin veil had been draped over her head and hung down over her face as they all awaited the arrival of Jack with Ormonde under arrest.

As the police coach turned right towards Kemble Station at the junction of Sandpool Lane with the main street, instead of turning left for the Swindon Road, Ormonde demanded an explanation.

'You asked to speak to a senior officer, did you not?' Jack reminded him with sadistic satisfaction. 'He's waiting to speak to you at Kemble Station, then it'll be all stations to Newgate.'

Back at the station, Percy was anxiously peering out from the darkness of the Booking Hall for any sign of the approaching coach, while Michael Parsons was fuming quietly from his chair inside the office, wondering how he was going to explain any passenger complaints to the Regional Inspector. Then from the outside door Percy heard two bells ringing inside the same room, where Lucy was waiting silently, eyes closed, in front of the covered mirror, praying for it all to be over so that she could discard the malodorous costume. The sweat smell from previous actresses under the armpits of a queenly gown was one thing, but this was unbearable.

Both she and Frances had jumped at the sound of the two rings of the bell inside the office and were glad when Percy rushed back in and glared at Michael Parsons.

'What was that ringing noise?' he demanded.

Parsons seemed not to be concerned. 'Two rings, sir. That's from the "down" signal box the other side of the bridge, to alert us that the London-bound through train just passed the box. It'll be here in a couple of minutes or so.'

Percy made it back out through the darkness of the Booking Hall as far as the door, where he saw the police coach pulling up in the forecourt and Ormonde being assisted out of it towards the station entrance. Percy rushed back inside the office and hissed for the action to begin when he gave the signal by dropping his outstretched arm, hoping upon hope that Jack made the agreed noise upon entry with his prisoner.

'In here, matey,' Percy heard Jack yell sarcastically and he dropped his arm. Frances swiftly and deftly whisked the covering blanket off the front of the mirror in the office and a ghostly face appeared on cue in the upper right hand corner of the Booking Hall. It shimmered in the half light, a funereal veil draped over a white face with black caverns where there should have been eyes and Ormonde screamed.

'Get that way from me!' he pleaded.

'What would that be?' Jack enquired calmly over the rumbling sound of the approaching train as it glided slowly past the platform in a cloud of steam that wafted into the Booking Hall and somehow added to the ghostly unreality of the merciless image hovering halfway up the wall.

'Leave me alone!' Ormonde pleaded hysterically. 'Go back to your grave! All I did was take your life in one short push, but you're going to haunt me for the rest of my days! Get out of my life — I'll be dead soon anyway! For God's sake leave me be!'

With the strength of a madman in mortal terror, he struggled free from the uncertain grasp of a Sergeant Oakley who was equally transfixed by the ghostly face that had appeared out of thin air, not having been warned in advance. Ormonde raced through onto the platform, skidded to the right and ran down its full length, leaving the end of the "up" platform at high speed and running around the guard's van of the London-bound train onto the "down" line.

The noise of the arriving London-bound train had masked the sound of a goods train destined for Cheltenham loaded with coal. It had reached its maximum speed of forty miles an hour and the hundreds of tons behind the engine ensured that even though a horrified driver applied the brake with commendable speed, it was too late to prevent the front of the smoke box door hitting Ormonde a resounding blow to the head that delivered a merciful death before his body was tossed like a rag doll fifty feet down the line, where it was mangled almost beyond recognition as the engine screeched down the track after it, wheels locked under the force of the brake, but the latent weight of the load behind it, in wagons with no brakes, pushing it relentlessly forward.

Back at the station, Sergeant Oakley and Constable Jacks had raced after their man, but had been sufficiently behind him to avoid the oncoming goods train. Oakley could see the fate that had befallen Ormonde from the end of the up platform and he turned to instruct his constable to fetch a lantern and check that their man was dead. Then the two men walked slowly back along the up line to where the goods train had finally ground to a halt on the other line and a trembling driver was in the process of descending from his cab.

'Can I get out of this disgusting costume now?' Lucy demanded, and the moment that Frances confirmed that she could, she raced back to the Ladies' Waiting Room to change back into her own clothes. Percy walked onto the platform and looked back down to where Oakley and Jacks were approaching the twisted remains wedged under the front wheels and he saw the young constable lean forward, then stagger sideways and spew all over the up line.

'I think we'll leave that to the local force,' he advised Jack.

Chapter Eighteen

'Well, that went *very* well, didn't it?' Chief Inspector Wallace bellowed sarcastically at the two men across the desk from him in his office at Scotland Yard. 'It cost us over a hundred pounds and we have no-one to put in front of a jury!'

Percy simply looked defiant, while Jack hung his head, red-faced and wishing he were somewhere else.

'We got our man,' Percy reminded him, but this was not about to stem the flow of wrath.

'We're supposed to buckle them, lock them up, bring them before a judge and jury, then hang them!' Wallace yelled back. 'Or have you become a public executioner as well? If so, let me remind you, the approved apparatus is a noose, not a coal train!'

'If we'd put him through the court process, some glib-tongued barrister might have got him off,' Percy offered by way of justification.

'Talking of expert use of the English language, read *that*!' Wallace thundered, as he reached forward, picked up that morning's copy of *The Times*, and hurled it back down in front of Percy.

'I already have, sir,' Percy confirmed, 'but that's just scurrilous uninformed rubbish.'

'The sort of scurrilous uninformed rubbish that's on the breakfast table of every Member of the House, let me remind you,' Wallace spat back. At least the volume had decreased, if the sentiment hadn't softened. Wallace glared at Jack. 'Do you have nothing to say, Constable?'

'We had no idea the man would make a run for it, sir,' Jack mumbled at the floor, provoking a bitter laugh.

'And he *wouldn't* have done, if either of you had secured him properly! Instead you pulled a cheap theatrical stunt designed to provoke him into a confession.'

'We got the confession, sir,' Percy reminded him, generating another angry outburst.

'And we can make precious little use of it now, can we, you pair of idiots! Is there something in your common inheritance that causes you to be feeble minded? Was a distant ancestor perhaps the village idiot?'

'My father — and Constable Enright's grandfather — was a doctor, as it happens,' Percy replied.

'Presumably not one who ministered to afflictions of the brain,' Wallace retorted, 'or else he would have had half his family committed!'

'The business with the train was just an unfortunate accident,' Percy observed.

'Unfortunate for your suspect, certainly. And we only have your word for it that he confessed before he ended it all in that spectacular fashion. *The Times* is suggesting that the two of you hounded him to suicide by staging some sort of séance, and the directors of the Great Western Railway have been obliged to publish a notice in the newspapers, assuring the travelling public that none of their lines are haunted!'

It fell silent for a moment, until Wallace held up a buff file and waved it in the air. 'My superiors have instructed me to go easy on you two because of your success in putting a stop to those prostitute murders in Whitechapel. But from what I can deduce from that file, you managed to kill the principal suspect in that case as well, didn't you?'

'That was me, sir,' Jack admitted. 'I hit her over the head with my billy club to prevent her slitting the throat of her latest victim.'

'Who, one can only hope, was *not* a prostitute, since you went on to marry her, did you not?'

'Yes, sir,' Jack admitted, unsure whether or not to remind him that he had been the one who had authorised Esther's involvement in this latest debacle. He decided against it, since they were in enough trouble already.

After another excruciatingly long silence, Wallace looked at each of them in turn before announcing his own verdict. 'I think it's high time we split up this unhealthy family enterprise of yours, killing suspects rather than arresting them. You, Constable, were allocated to your uncle's team because it was felt that you would benefit most from an avuncular influence. That was a very grave mistake on someone's part, it would seem, and I've marked on both your files that you're never to be allowed out of London together on the same case ever again. That leaves the question of your next allocations.'

They waited in a deathly silence that Wallace employed to maximum effect before continuing. 'Constable, you'll be allocated to general duties in Inspector Pennington's team. I'm not sure what they have on at the moment, but they'll shortly be kicking down doors in Limehouse in search of Chinese drug dens and the like. As for you, Sergeant, we need promoted men to boost the squad investigating a series of bank robberies that we believe may all be the work of the same gang. If you discover that they are, Chief Superintendant Murphy would be grateful if you'd leave a few of them alive for him to buckle. Very well, out you go, the pair of you.'

'Look on the bright side, young Jack,' Percy grinned unrepentantly as they headed downstairs to the canteen. 'Your mother will be delighted that you're out from under my wicked influence and Esther will have a greater expectation of your being home for tea on time every evening.'

'Do you still have a job, or will I have to start taking washing in?' Esther asked as she wrapped her arms around Jack in the hallway when he returned home.

'Only mine,' Jack grinned sheepishly at her, 'but I'm afraid I won't be working with Uncle Percy any more.'

'And that's *bad* news?' Esther replied with a gleeful smile. 'You must be the only one left in the family who's got any remaining faith in him. Your mother thinks he's the Anti-Christ, and when I visited Lucy today she could talk about nothing but the stinking dress he forced her to climb into in order to scare the pants off Ormonde. As for me, you presumably haven't forgotten what I had to go through as the result of his hair-brained scheme?'

'You're right about Mother,' Jack agreed. 'She'll be over the moon, until she learns that my immediate duties are likely to bring me face to face with drug-drenched Chinamen wielding hatchets.'

'Don't tell her that, else she'll resume her never-ending campaign to persuade you to resign from the police force. And I might even join her in that.'

It fell silent as Jack looked down into her eyes with a pleading look. 'Do you *really* want me to give it up and become a coalman?'

She softened and kissed the end of his nose. 'What, and create even more washing for me? It's what you want to do and what you were doing when we first met. It's how we got together.'

'Yes, and that nearly got you killed as well,' Jack reminded her. 'If I've learned one lesson, it's never to allow you to get involved in my work again.'

'*Allow* me?' Esther bridled. 'You're not my father, Jack — if I want to get involved in something, I will, with or without your permission. And now I need to get involved in preparing supper.'

'That's something else,' Jack admitted hesitantly. 'It's taken care of.'

'You're taking me to supper at the Cafe Royal?' Esther asked sarcastically.

'Not exactly — but I've arranged for more of that fried fish and potatoes to be delivered.'

Esther's brow knitted in a frown. 'Since when did Farringdon Market tradesmen deliver to your home?'

'They don't,' Jack conceded, and Esther's eyes flew wide open as the realisation hit her.

'Not Uncle Percy? He wouldn't dare show his face in here after what he got us into, and damned near ended your career.'

'He's not turning up alone, so please be nice to him,' Jack pleaded.

'*Nice* to him?' Esther echoed. 'I'll scream at him if he comes within ten feet of our front door! So who's he bringing with him — the Police Commissioner?'

'Next best thing — Aunt Beattie.'

'I'm surprised she's still married to him, after all those years of madcap bungling.'

'He's actually a very good thief catcher,' Jack offered in his defence.

'Oh, so it's only murderers he kills, is that it?'

'You'd better get yourself beautified in order to receive our supper guests,' Jack suggested.

'You mean I don't look beautiful now, in my apron, with my hair in pins and no makeup?'

'Of course you do, but I know that you women like to look your best in the company of others.'

'It's as well that I agreed to marry you, Jack Enright, because you know nothing about women,' Esther insisted, just as the knock came on the front door. 'You might have given me more notice than this! Keep them entertained while I go and smarten myself up.' She scuttled down to the bedroom, leaving Jack to open the door to their visitors, accept the steaming parcel from a beaming Aunt Beatrice and the wine bottle from Uncle Percy, and lead them down to the kitchen, where the food was placed in the oven to keep it warm, and Aunt Beatrice made a bee-line for the nursery in order to make a big fuss over 'the darling little Lily that I so rarely see'.

A few minutes later Esther reappeared just as Jack was opening the wine bottle. She had rapidly transformed herself into the elegant hostess, wearing her best maternity gown that still didn't quite disguise the burgeoning bump below her navel. She threw her arms around Aunt Beatrice and scowled at Percy behind her back. Then she made a show of rearranging the supper table after Jack's inadequate efforts to lay it and invited everyone to take a seat.

'Percy tells me that you to won't be working together any more,' Beattie commented by way of a silence breaker.

'At least that'll improve his chances of staying alive,' Esther replied sarcastically, but Percy wasn't going to let her get away with that.

'You think so? Opium is big business down near the docks and our Oriental friends don't take kindly to our interrupting their trade.'

'When exactly are you due?' Beattie asked Esther, hoping to divert the conversation.

'Are they really as violent as I've heard?' Jack persisted.

'Sometime in June, according to the doctor,' Esther replied across the male conversation.

'Not simply violent — crafty as well,' Percy advised Jack. 'They have to regularly change the men on the opium den details because the Chinese who operate them are not above bribery and threats. And they're particularly good at hiding their true activities behind lawful ones.'

'Are you two going to talk police work all evening?' Beattie demanded. 'I thought that would be an end to it, when they split you two up. Apparently not.'

'I'm simply warning Jack about what he's going to be up against in his next set of duties,' Percy insisted.

Jack was all ears. 'Have you had much experience of that sort of thing, Uncle?'

'Some years ago,' Percy replied as he stared nostalgically at the far wall. 'It was when I first joined the Yard, after working out of Bow Street, and they thought that my experience among the totties and street sharpsters might be of some value. There was a set of premises in Gerrard Street, Soho, which we suspected of operating a pipe house. To outward appearances it was only a restaurant, but when we entered one night we found a gambling room at the back. The proprietor was all smiles and bows when we nicked him for that, then it occurred to my boss at the time that Mr Ho was not looking unhappy enough. So we went upstairs, where we found his bawdy house. He still didn't look totally devastated, so we tried the next floor, and that was an eye-opener, believe me.'

'Percy,' Beattie intervened in a warning tone, but it was too late in the tale to stop him.

'Go on,' Jack invited him, and Percy obliged.

'Imagine a large room with no widows, just rows of beds down either side, men — and a couple of women as well — lying there almost insensible, with a couple of girls moving backwards and forwards between them, handing them pipes full of what turned out to be opium. Mr Ho was shouting and jumping up and down by that stage, so we knew we'd finally hit his weak spot. He offered my boss hundreds of pounds to turn a blind eye and offered the rest of us the pick of his whores one floor down, but the last I heard our generous host was still in Newgate, serving a very long stretch.'

'Right, that's it!' Beattie announced. 'Either you change the subject or we're leaving now.'

'Actually,' Esther intervened with a related topic, 'I was hoping you could advise us what's happened to poor Abigail Prendergast at Ormonde's art gallery. She and I got quite friendly when I worked there and I know that she was dependent on her job to continue her art studies. Is she going to be alright?'

Percy nodded as he began filling his after supper pipe. 'I called in there last week, to advise her of the date of the inquest, which incidentally is *next* week, in Kemble. I'll have to be there, obviously, but the bulk of the evidence will be coming from Sergeant Oakley, thank God. Anyway, Miss Prendergast won't need to attend, but she advised me that Ormonde has a cousin who's an antique dealer and he's bought the premises from the estate. The initial plan is to keep the gallery running, with Miss Prendergast as its manageress, so Ormonde's death worked very much in her favour.'

'Which is more than be said for you two,' Esther reminded them. 'Did you really expect that the spiriting up of his sister's ghost would result in a confession?'

'Well it did, didn't it?' Percy replied with a smile.

'But Ormonde's death?' Esther persisted. 'Was that all part of your master plan?'

'Of course not. It was genuinely an unfortunate turn of events.'

'You realise that you have a reputation in the Yard for killing your suspects?' Jack told him and Percy smiled.

'That won't do me any harm. You'll be aware of the general attitude in there — provided we get the villain, nobody cares how it comes about.'

'But there are procedures laid down by law, surely?' Esther insisted and Beattie snorted.

'Percy never follows procedure. I well remember that when we got married, he kept the ring in his own jacket pocket because he didn't trust his best man with it.'

'Well, he *was* in the Robbery Squad,' Percy replied with a chuckle. 'But he was also one of the most forgetful officers I ever knew. If anyone could be relied upon to dive out of a police wagon minus his billy staff it was Tommy Fletcher. "Forgetful Fletcher", we used to call him. It killed him in the end — he forgot to duck when the bullets started flying during an armed robbery in Holloway.'

'Horrible!' Esther muttered and Beattie smiled across at her sympathetically.

'Welcome to the Scotland Yard Apprentice Widows' Club, Esther. If Jack's anything like his uncle — which, let me assure you, he is — then nothing will persuade him to give up police work and find a less dangerous job. Anyway, I'd better take Percy home before he persuades Jack to undertake firearms training.'

'You get an extra three bob a week for that,' Jack announced thoughtfully. Esther smacked him across the back of his head and Percy and Beattie made their farewells with the usual hugs and undertakings not to leave it so long until their next gathering.

'And you take care of that lovely wife of yours,' Beattie instructed Jack just before the front door closed behind them.

Esther turned quickly and hugged Jack to her.

'You really *won't* volunteer to use a gun, just for an extra three shillings a week, will you?'

'Of course not. Aunt Beattie was just having you on. She's spent the last thirty years living on the edge of her seat waiting for the news that Uncle Percy's copped it in the line of duty.'

'And me?' Esther said with tears forming in her eyes. 'Is that *my* future, as well? Waiting for the knock on the door?'

'Your future, my darling wife,' Jack assured her as he hugged her closer, 'is to be loved to death by a husband who adores you, and raise two beautiful children in relative comfort. If you're definitely finished with detective work?'

'Until next time, knowing you,' Esther replied as she leaned forward and kissed him.

A NOTE TO THE READER

I hope that you enjoyed this third novel in the Esther and Jack series; if you've already read the first two, then you're obviously as hooked on the events in the life of this engaging family as I am. The only difference between us is that they've chosen me as their literary agent, and everything they do comes into my head first.

In this third volume I felt obliged to remind the reader that as the Nineteenth Century was drawing to a close, the work of Scotland Yard was not confined to London. What had begun as an experiment in criminal detection in the 1840s had expanded by the final decade of Victoria's reign into one of the world's most organised and effective crime detection organisations, and it was in great demand.

Not every police force had its own Detective Branch of plainclothes officers who were free of routine patrol work, and could therefore concentrate instead on stealthy enquiries in their own clothes, disguised if necessary as workmen, tradespeople or professionals. The rural forces in particular did not develop what we now call 'CID' branches until relatively recently, and if they were called upon to investigate something out of the routine, such as a murder or a serial sex offender, they would call in 'The Yard'.

Those of us old enough to have been reared on slightly cheesy TV series such as 'Fabian of The Yard' retain a vague memory of serious looking individuals in trilby hats, smoking pipes as they were driven through the streets in black sedans with bells ringing loudly to warn other motorists, and pedestrians, that a serious crime had been committed, and that the elite professionals were on their way to 'crack' it.

It was no different – although the ubiquitous black motor sedan was not yet available – for Yard officers in the 1890s, who were frequently transferred from their normal duties suppressing crime in London in order to assist a rural force that possessed no detectives. Thus it was that Percy and Jack Enright found themselves in deepest Wiltshire, looking for a reason why a young woman finished up dead inside a railway tunnel. But once it was discovered that the victim came from an up-market location in London, they had need of the services of their third, and highly unofficial, team member, Esther, who was already feeling mentally unfulfilled while settling into the traditional role of the late Victorian wife and mother.

The storyline of this novel is also different in another vital respect. Whereas detective work traditionally involves a search for a culprit, this time Jack and Percy have no doubt as to his identity almost from the start of their investigations. What they are required to search for on this occasion is the evidence to prove it, and Esther is soon undertaking lines of enquiry of her own. Undercover, of course, since officially she doesn't occupy any role in the work of the Metropolitan Police – no woman would, until well after the turn of the century.

Percy is an old hand at the use of techniques that are not so much 'undercover' as downright 'underhand', and he doesn't shrink from using a cheap theatrical trick. This *was* the age of optical illusion, after all, and although the moving picture was still a thing of the future, audiences formed long queues to marvel at stills photography and kaleidoscopic effects, while gasping in awe at the antics of stage performers such as Harry Houdini and sitting around chilly tables beneath red lamps while mediums, both genuine and fake, connected them with the spirit world. Who, therefore, can blame Percy for resorting to 'Pepper's Ghost', which was already thirty years old by then?

As ever, I'd be delighted to receive your feedback, in addition to your requests regarding what the Enrights should tackle next. In their next two novels they will be back in London, but always happy to pack their bags and move on somewhere else. I would be delighted if you could post a review up on **Amazon** or **Goodreads**. Or, of course, you can try the more personal approach on my website, and my Facebook page: **DavidFieldAuthor**.

Happy reading!

David

davidfieldauthor.com

Sapere Books is an exciting new publisher of brilliant fiction and popular history.

To find out more about our latest releases and our monthly bargain books visit our website:
saperebooks.com

Printed in Great Britain
by Amazon

36674138R00109